If You Ever Come Back

K. L. SAWYER

For the hearts that got a little lost along the way,
love will always know where to find you.

Playlist

If You Ever Come Back - *The Script*
The Man Who Can't be Moved - *The Script*
The Last Time - *The Script*
Breakeven - *The Script*
Never Seen Anything Quite Like You - *The Script*
Sing - *Travis*
I Can't Make You Love Me – *Bon Iver*
Thinking of You - *Katy Perry*
Cardigan - *Taylor Swift*
August - *Taylor Swift*
Delicate - *Taylor Swift*
You and Me - *Lifehouse*
Never Say Never - *The Fray*
Look After You - *The Fray*
You Found Me - *The Fray*
Chasing Cars - *Snow Patrol*
She Will Be Loved - *Maroon 5*
Here's to the Night - *Eve 6*
Somewhere Only We Know - *Keane*
Yellow - *Coldplay*
Sparks - *Coldplay*

She (For Liz) - *Parachute*
The Mess I Made - *Parachute*
Kiss Me Slowly - *Parachute*
Best Intentions - *Hodera*
Why Can't I - *Liz Phair*
Greta Van Fleet - *Light My Love*
Portland, Maine - *Donovan Woods*
Turning Page – *Sleeping at Last*
Flightless Bird, American Mouth – *Iron and Wine*
Mess – *Noah Kahan*
Crazier Things (with Noah Kahan) – *Chelsea Cutler*

Prologue

KEIRA

"Whatever our souls are made of, his and mine are the same."
— Emily Brontë

Love is not always loud. Sometimes, it whispers across decades, slipping between cracks in memory, carried in the quiet of a song you haven't heard in years or the smell of salt on late summer air. It lives in the breath between sentences, in the silence after goodbyes.

It is the ache of what could have been.

The softness of a name you haven't spoken in so long, it feels unfamiliar in your mouth.

It's the letter you never sent. The book you borrowed and meant to return.

Sometimes it changes shape, growing out of childhood promises and into something raw and complicated. Sometimes it hurts. And sometimes it disappears altogether, slipping into the blur of becoming who you're meant to be.

And for some, their love stories don't end.

They just took the long way home.

Chapter 1

KEIRA

❄

THEN — AGE 24

PORTLAND, MAINE

I didn't know this would be the last time we'd see each other.

Not really. I mean; I guess that maybe deep down I knew something was ending. But I didn't think this was it, at least not for us.

We were sitting on the back steps of my childhood home, the porch light softly buzzing above us, flickering like it couldn't decide whether to stay on.

It was a particularly chilly night. The kind of late October air that hinted snow wasn't far off, but not enough to drive us inside. The air smelled like fresh firewood, drifting from nearby chimneys, and the whole street felt steeped in fall, like it always did this time of year.

Our neighbors had lined their porches with carved pumpkins and trick-or-treat bowls, while others tied bundles of dried corn to their front doors. Posters of the annual fall festival hung on telephone poles and inside coffee shops.

It should've felt cozy and familiar, but all I could think while looking up at the night sky was how dark it was. Darker than I'd seen it in a while.

Looking back, it had been fitting for the occasion.

Miles kept tapping his thumb against his knee, like he was trying to distract himself from the inevitable.

"So…when's your flight?" I asked, even though I already knew the answer.

"Seven."

It was already after midnight, and I knew he wouldn't be sleeping tonight. Neither of us would.

I nodded, staring at the edge of the step. "Are you all packed?" He gave a small nod in return and kept tapping.

I wanted to ask him not to go. I wanted to say *stay, or what if we could figure this out, or choose me.* But I decided against it.

Because this job in Chicago was everything he'd worked for. And because I loved him enough to let him go. Too bad I'd never had the courage to tell him that to his face.

He finally spoke. "I was going to call instead of showing up. I didn't think you wanted…" He stopped himself. "I didn't think I'd see you."

A small, sad smile formed at the corners of my mouth. "And since when are you the type not to randomly show up on my doorstep?"

That got a chuckle out of him, but it was gone quicker than it came.

"Did you want to see me?" I asked softly.

"Yeah," he said. "Of course I did. I always want to."

That made my throat close. I looked away.

"I want you to know that I really am happy for you," I said, even though it hurt. "You deserve this."

"I guess. It just doesn't feel the way I thought it would."

"Why not?"

4

"Honestly? Because you're not coming with me."

I didn't have an answer for that. Not one I could say out loud without sounding slightly pathetic. Besides, I had my own dreams. My own goals. My entire life was still here, and his was already packed into a suitcase.

The truth was, Miles and I never seemed to get the timing right. We hovered in that space between friendship and something more for years, neither of us brave enough to cross the line into a real relationship. As for me, I was held back by fear. If we tried and fell apart, I'd lose him entirely, and that was a risk I couldn't bring myself to take.

I was a coward. In every sense of the word.

He reached out like he was going to touch my hand but pulled back at the last second. "I don't know how to leave you."

"But you are." It came out sharper than I wanted.

His eyes flicked to mine. "You're always going to be my best friend, Keira."

I took a deep breath. The word friend lingered in the air, turning my stomach. Last time I checked, "friends" didn't sleep together. They didn't spend time wondering if they were ever going to be something more. But this wasn't the time for me to be selfish.

"This will be a good thing for you, it's an opportunity you've been waiting for, Miles, and I won't stand in the way of that," I said. My head dropped slightly, and I was suddenly staring at my shoes. "You don't have to worry about me. I'll be fine." There it was. The pause.

The moment where everything could shift. Where someone finally says what they meant, and it changes everything.

But he didn't say anything. And neither did I.

"Well…I should get going," he said. "Early flight and all."

"Miles—"

"Yeah?"

I opened my mouth, but nothing came out.

He waited, then gave a small, heartbroken smile before placing his hand gently against my cheek. He touched his lips to mine in an all too familiar kiss that ended far too soon.

"I'll see you," he said.

I nodded, though I think we both knew better. I hadn't realized we'd been holding hands until he slipped out of mine.

He walked down the steps and didn't look back.

I stayed there long after he was gone, trying to convince myself I'd done the right thing by letting him go. That love, real love, didn't ask someone to give up who they are.

But I couldn't help but feel like I'd just made a huge mistake, and in that moment, I truly felt like I'd lost something I wasn't going to get back.

***

FIVE YEARS LATER

ROCKPORT, MASSACHUSETTS

Dylan was still asleep when I got up.

I kicked the covers off me, only now realizing we forgot to lower the heat last night before heading up to bed. Dylan liked to keep the windows shut, whereas I liked the air, even in the dead of winter. We never really argued about it, so instead, we'd just take turns on who'd win that day.

I slipped out of bed quietly and tiptoed past Lola, our Australian Shepherd, who lifted her head and gave me a single thump of her tail before settling back down.

"Good girl," I whispered as I gave her a soft pat.

I padded over to the closet and pulled out my usual work outfit: comfortable black leggings and my favorite sweater dress. As I tugged the dress over my head, I caught my reflection in the mirror. My dark brown hair was slightly tangled from sleep, and my deep brown eyes still had that soft, just-woken-up look.

I didn't bother with much makeup, just a quick swipe of mascara and my favorite tinted lip balm from the counter. I was on the shorter side, but I liked my freckles and the way my hair waved when it air-dried. I didn't mind how I looked and thought my style suited me well enough, even if I tended to feel plain next to most girls.

I turned from the mirror and grabbed my wool scarf with its matching beanie and was about to head to work when I heard Dylan mumble something, half asleep. He rolled onto his stomach, getting more comfortable.

I leaned against the door frame and watched him for a second. His hair had fallen messily across his forehead, and one leg was sprawled out from beneath the blanket. He always looked so comfortable when he slept.

I loved him, of course. How could I not?

He was kind and reliable and made me coffee every morning when I was running late. He took the time to ask me about my day and would bring me my favorite takeout on his way home from work as a surprise.

He'd been in my life for three years, and nothing about it was wrong. He never raised his voice, he remembered to ask about my deadlines, and most importantly, he always, always, laughed at my terrible impressions of Jane Austen characters.

Our relationship was good. It was safe. But sometimes I found myself wondering in secret whether safety was what I truly wanted. And lately, with the wedding date officially set for next spring, I'd felt myself pulling back without meaning to. It felt like a quiet distance I couldn't explain, not even to myself.

I felt a soft smile spread as I took one last look at him before making my way to the living room. I pushed open the large bay windows that faced the harbor and let the crisp morning air rush in.

The scent of salt and sea filled the room instantly, clean and comforting. I let the breeze play with my hair while I looked out onto the harbor, breathing it all in. It was my favorite scent in the world. It always had a way of filling me up from the inside and giving me goosebumps.

It's difficult to explain to those who have never felt it, but all I can tell you is that it smelled like home.

In the kitchen, I moved through my routine like muscle memory. For once, I'd started my day on time, so I turned on the coffee pot, got some toast going, fed Lola, and checked the weather. Snow was in the forecast for later, but for now, the sunlight broke through the gray clouds just enough to warm the edge of the counter, casting a soft, golden glow across the surface.

I grabbed my keys and slid on my fur-lined boots. My phone buzzed with a reminder about a vendor order for the shop. Another buzz came shortly after regarding the looming manuscript deadline.

I rolled my eyes and told myself to ignore both, just for now. I wasn't trying to be avoidant. I just had so much on my plate lately that everything felt like it was piling up at once, and I was scared it wouldn't take much for all of it to spill over.

I walked down the back stairs to the cozy little bookshop I'd bought on a whim after years of saving. I had been an aspiring writer my whole life and figured I'd have to start somewhere. So, I bought the place from my dad's friend for a deal, and it just happened to include an upstairs apartment.

It couldn't have worked out better.

I live in the coastal town of Rockport, Massachusetts. I grew up not far from here and spent most of my summers playing on these beaches, so it was an obvious choice for me.

Bearskin Neck is a well-known peninsula that always slows down in the winter. Spring and summer bring crowds, and on busy days, tourists shuffle past the window with cups of melting ice cream and shopping bags from the art galleries and saltwater taffy shops.

The air always smelled like salt and sometimes even fish if the harbor had been active. And on quiet mornings, the streets were still. Just the creak of old signs swaying in the sea breeze and the soft sound of waves hitting the rocks. Those were my favorite days.

My bookstore was tucked between a knick-knack shop that sold hand-painted buoys and a café with the best clam chowder I'd ever tasted. The building was old with slanted floors, weathered beams, and creaky doors, but that's what I love about it. It had character.

There was a reading nook I set up by the front window with a mismatched armchair I managed to grab from a thrift shop. A throw blanket and a bowl of pine-scented potpourri lay next to my favorite cinnamon candle on the oak side table.

From the front window of the shop, I could see the tip of the jetty and, if I leaned just right, Motif No. 1. To the tourists, it was the iconic red fishing shack everyone paints, photographs, and buys postcards of. To me, it was a reminder of who I was and who I'd always be—a small-town coastal girl.

This year, I'd decided to decorate with a Christmas tree made from donated books I received over the last year. I strung twinkling lights over it and placed fake presents underneath. I was very proud of that tree; you could ask anyone.

It sat in the front corner by the window in all its glory, welcoming customers with that warm Christmas spirit.

Most days, I opened early, played something soft on the old speakers, and drank my coffee before anyone else stepped inside. The shop was small, quiet, and mine.

And most days, it was enough.

The town hadn't been fully awake yet as I unlocked the front door and stepped in, the little bell above me jingling happily. I'd left a candle burning too long the day before, and the scent of it had soaked into everything, staining the place with thick cinnamon.

I opened the window, letting it air out a bit, and instantly felt the cold pressed against my skin; it was colder than it had been all week, but I didn't mind.

If I'm honest, winter was always my favorite. The ocean held a thin layer of ice along the edges, and the air carried that unmistakable scent of snow. Everything felt softer. Still. The gray skies, the quiet streets. It was always its own kind of magic.

I dropped my bag behind the counter, flipped the "Closed" sign to "Open," and stood there for a second, just listening.

It was one of those rare moments when everything was calm, and I wanted to soak that in as much as I could before the customers began arriving.

I slid into my seat behind the counter, taking a slow sip of coffee as I sifted through the stack of papers waiting for me. When I glanced up, my eyes landed on the first dollar bill the shop ever earned, still taped to the register with the note my mom had written. She'd insisted on being my very first customer.

Things between us hadn't always been easy, but she'd worked hard to repair what had been broken, and I realized how much I wanted that too. Her support now means more to me than I ever expected.

The bell above the door chimed around noon. I lifted my head briefly and gave them a warm greeting. A woman entered first, tall and blond and bundled up in a stylish peacoat. Behind her was a man—broad-shouldered, dark hair, sunglasses and a hoodie pulled up underneath his jean jacket.

They seemed comfortable in the way couples get when they've known each other for years.

I could easily tell they weren't from here and was surprised to see tourists this late in the year, but money was money, and I couldn't be happier to have some customers.

The woman wandered toward the fiction wall while the man stopped by the local interest table.

I went back to organizing the bookmarks I had in front of me while they browsed.

"Hey, Miles!" the woman called from across the shop, holding up a book. "Didn't you read this one?"

My eyes lifted before I could stop them.

And for a second, my hands froze on the stack of bookmarks.

I didn't mean to look up. It was automatic, like the name hit a nerve I didn't know was still exposed.

I knew it wasn't him. I didn't even have to look twice. But for half a second, the possibility hung in the air...what if it was?

What would I say? What would he do?

When the rush faded and my heart stopped racing, all that was left was the dull, familiar ache of disappointment.

I shook it off.

It was just a name. That's all it was.

I slid the bookmarks back into place, straightened out the rest of the counter, and told myself to get a grip. I wasn't seventeen anymore. I have a life now. I had a business, a fiancé, and a dog that waited for me to come home.

I got up and poured the rest of my second cup of coffee down the sink, suddenly not in the mood for it anymore, and went to restock the poetry shelf.

The couple didn't stay long. They bought a mug and a travel guide to New England. She smiled as she paid, and he held the door open for her on the way out.

And just like that, my day continued as normal.

***

I closed shop around 6 p.m.

Just as I was locking the front door, a buzz came from my pocket. Dylan had sent me a text letting me know he was running late from the office. That had been fine with me. I mostly enjoyed my solitude, especially after a workday.

Dylan worked as an urban planner. Most of his jobs involved green city initiatives, walkability projects, and things like that. He cared about people, about the environment, and about making things better in ways most people never even thought about.

It was one of the things I admired most about him. He believed in building something good, something that would last.

I decided to take a walk instead of heading upstairs. My favorite café's lights were still lit, so I decided to pop in, suddenly craving something sweet.

The bell chimed over the door as I opened it, the warm air hitting me right in the face.

The girl at the front looked up briefly before going right back to work on an order. "Hey, Keira, the usual?" she said

"Actually, I feel like switching it up tonight. Can you whip me up a London Fog?"

A smile edged at the corner of her mouth. "You know I can."

"Thanks, Lucy."

She always made a great hot chocolate, which was my usual go-to. She would use this homemade marshmallow whipped topping instead of regular store-bought whipped cream and it was like heaven to a cocoa lover, such as myself.

While I waited, I treated myself to a scoop of their house-made pistachio gelato, my favorite, and savored it in the quiet as I watched the Christmas lights twinkle along the windows of the neighboring shops.

"Order up, Keira." Lucy handed me the cup with a warm smile before adding, "Hey, how's that new book coming along?"

"Oh, you know, it's going as well as it could," I said, while keeping how I truly felt to myself.

Awful. Horrible. Exhausting. Sucking the absolute life out of me.

I grabbed my drink and headed out back into the cold. I walked out to the jetty and took a seat on one of the large flat boulders by the edge. A huge Christmas tree had been built out of lobster traps at the end of the cul-de-sac and was decorated with colorful buoys and rainbow string lights. It was a tradition that most ocean-side towns did during the holidays, and one I never got tired of seeing.

I took a sip of my latte and looked out at the still black waters ahead, letting the winter air fill my lungs.

It had been a long time since I'd ordered this drink, so long in fact that I couldn't remember why I'd stopped. But tonight, it felt right. It was warm and comforting, somewhat nostalgic, and exactly what I needed.

The warmth settled in my hands, and my mind drifted somewhere else entirely—back to a version of myself who used to love nights like this, back when I didn't have the pressure of deadlines or the heaviness of life pressing down on me.

The quiet had a way of bringing up the things I'd buried deep, and as the wind curled around me, I felt that old ache surface again, uninvited and undeniable.

Chapter 2

MILES

❄

PRESENT DAY

CHICAGO, ILLINOIS

The meeting had been over for ten minutes, but I was still staring at the blueprint on the conference room wall like it held all the answers.

"Hey, man, I'm about to head out. You good here?" one of the new interns asked behind me.

I nodded without looking. "Yeah. I've got some stuff to finish up in here and think about going forward."

It was bullshit. I wasn't thinking about the blueprint.

The truth was, I couldn't even remember what we had decided on. Something about material costs and a timeline shift. I'd tuned out somewhere between the second coffee refill and the part where someone made a terrible dad joke about sleep being optional.

In truth, this had been just one of those days when I'd been overthinking: my life, what the hell I was doing with it, and where I saw myself going.

Most would call it a five-year plan. I just called it my five-year existential crisis.

Thinking wasn't doing me any good, as usual, so I left the conference room and walked the loop around the office, mostly out of habit.

I was constantly surrounded by the suffocating glass walls, the smell of stale coffee, and the low tapping of keyboards. I was in the office more than any person should be. I basically lived here at this point.

I was well known and respected as one of the lead architects. I was the guy who stayed late, who hit every deadline, who kept his head down and got shit done. I had no life outside of work, and it showed.

I made it back to my office and shut the door. The Chicago skyline stretched across the window, full of high rises that I helped create, the slow sprawl of an expanding city finding itself before me. I used to stare at it, feeling like I was chasing something. Now I just felt drained and bored.

My phone buzzed on the counter. It had come from a text attached to a name I didn't recognize:

> Sara: Hey! The other night was fun, we should do it again! Drinks tonight?

I stared at it for a moment, trying to place the name. A blurry face, maybe a brunette or…shit, was she blond? Nothing had been clear. I must have saved it the other night after one too many drinks.

I thought about it for a second, considering my options, and shrugged. What the hell, I thought to myself. I sent a quick text back before slipping my cell back into my pocket.

> Me: Sure, it's a date.

I swear I wasn't an asshole. I honestly think I'd just stopped caring.

There were others, of course. Dates, hookups, people who tried to get close—I'd let them in, but only so far. Just enough to pass the time.

Most of them blurred together between conversations that didn't go deeper than work, and someone slipping out of my apartment or me leaving theirs.

I tried to convince myself that I'd moved on, that this was normal. That I was just being careful this time. But the truth was simpler than that: no one ever stuck. No one ever made me feel anything close to what she had. And it wasn't fair to them that I compared them all to her. From little things like the way she looked at me, to slightly more personal things like the way being around her meant letting my guard fully down.

I'd had something real once, even if it was never really "official" in the traditional sense. And no matter how much I tried to pretend otherwise, I hadn't let it go. I wasn't sure I'd ever be able to.

I continued with my day and went through the motions. I answered a few emails, reviewed a materials list I'd already approved twice, and then I sat there, staring at the screen, hoping something—anything—would break the monotony.

But nothing came except a knock at the door. Before I could say anything, Ava leaned in. She was our project coordinator and had been incredibly good at pretending the stress didn't get to her. I envied her for that.

"Good morning, sunshine! The client meeting's been moved to Thursday. That gives you a little breathing room."

"Thanks," I said without looking up from my computer. Sunshine had become her new nickname for me since I'd been walking around with a storm cloud over my head as of late.

She lingered for a moment.

"You okay?" she asked.

I looked up. "Yeah. Why?"

She shrugged. "You just look like you haven't slept. Your vibe seems a little off today."

I had slept. Technically. Just not well.

"I'm fine," I said. "Just one of those days."

She studied me for another second, then her smile suddenly lit up. "If you're bored, you could always come to happy hour. Mason's trying to get the interns drunk again."

I gave a half-laugh. "I'll pass. I told you the last time you dragged me with you that I was never going out with the interns again."

"Yeah, I remember." She let out a deep sigh. "You know, one of these days, you're going to have to prove you're not actually a robot and come have fun with us."

I turned back toward my computer. "I prefer to keep myself a mystery."

She smirked and pulled the door shut behind her.

I leaned back in my chair after the door closed, letting the silence settle around me.

It wasn't that I didn't like people. I could be friendly when I needed to be, but making real connections, forming anything lasting, had never come easily.

I kept most people at arm's length. Coworkers, acquaintances, even old friends from back home. I told myself it was the job, the long hours, the constant demands that left no room for much else. And maybe that was part of it. But sometimes I wondered if I just didn't have it in me anymore. If somewhere along the way, I got used to the quiet, and now anything outside of it just felt like too much.

I looked down at the plans on my desk. Another high-end condo project near the lake. Sleek, modern, and efficient—exactly what the client wanted. Floor-to-ceiling windows. Minimalist design. Everything about it was polished and carefully controlled.

It was going to be beautiful. A success on paper.

But right then, none of it mattered. I couldn't remember the last time I had felt genuinely excited about something. I'd built a life full of structure and routine, but there were days it felt more like I was moving through it than living in it.

The office thinned out by six. People grabbed their bags, called elevators, and made their way toward the valet. I stayed behind another half hour to finish up the work I was doing.

There was a sharp chill in the air as I stepped outside. Night had settled fully over the city, the sky a deep, inky black, above the glow of streetlights and passing cars.

Sara had messaged me back earlier, letting me know when and where to meet her tonight. Since we weren't meeting until 9 p.m., I decided to take the long way home, letting my feet carry me through the quieter streets.

As I walked, I took it all in. The towering buildings, the rhythm of traffic, the way the city never really slept. It was moments like this, surrounded by the busy sounds of the city, when I would think about home.

***

Growing up in Portland was quiet and familiar. It was the kind of place where people knew your name, where your teachers had gone to school with your parents, and you ran into the same faces at the grocery store, the library, and the beach.

Summers were short but good, and consisted of late nights by the water, cheap ice cream, and walking home with sand in your shoes.

Winters were long and cold, and it felt like the town was put on pause, especially when the snow started to fall. But there was a rhythm to it, a sense of consistency that made everything feel comfortable.

Chicago was the opposite in almost every way. It was fast, unpredictable, always pushing forward. No one stopped to ask how you'd been. Things were constantly changing. New buildings were being erected, new faces were everywhere you looked, and all sorts of pop-up shops came and went every month.

It kept you on your toes, but sometimes it was exhausting. And I couldn't help but miss the way Portland felt like it knew me personally.

I tried to shake it off. Yeah, I missed it. I missed home more than

I wanted to admit. I missed the way my mom always had a hot meal waiting whenever I drove home from college, as if she'd been listening for my car to pull into the driveway. I missed how my dad and I would wrestle with the Christmas lights while she stood on the porch insisting they were crooked, even when they weren't. But I'd worked too damn hard to get here. Letting that kind of feeling in would only make the distance from them harder to live with, and I wasn't ready to deal with all of that yet.

After stopping home to shower and change, I headed back out to meet Sara. She chose a little wine bar in the West Loop that I'd never been to. It had been decorated with warm lights and black leather booths and was the kind of place where people dressed up nice regardless of what day it was.

She waved when she saw me walk in. I was glad she at least remembered what I looked like.

"Hey," she said, standing to give me a quick hug. "You look nice."

"Thanks," I replied, unbuttoning my coat. "You do too."

She wore a long, dark coat and, underneath, a long black dress that fit her well. Her outfit was the perfect mix of casual and upscale, which made her fit right in here. Her makeup was simple but done well, and her hair curled out at the ends.

She looked good; there was no denying that. At least drunk-me still had taste.

We walked in and took a seat at one of the leather booths. The conversation started easily enough. She was smart. Confident. Pretty in a polished, sure-of-herself kind of way.

Shortly after, a waitress came over and took our order. We'd both gone simple: a glass of cabernet and the rigatoni with spicy vodka sauce for her, while I went with the grilled salmon with roasted vegetables and a tall beer on tap. The food looked good when it arrived, so I told myself that it was a win.

I offered a quick smile as the waitress walked off. "You picked a solid spot."

Sara grinned. "Thanks. I come here with friends sometimes. They do a great brunch."

I nodded and picked up my fork. "I'll have to try it."

It wasn't a lie. I could try brunch here sometime if the food held up.

She started in on her pasta, then glanced up. "So, big question...do you actually like your job? Or are you just good at pretending?"

I smirked, appreciative of the effort. "Depends on the day."

She laughed lightly. "Fair enough. Same here."

I chewed slowly, trying to hold the thread. "What is it you do again?"

"I'm an accountant for a law firm," she said. "I know, it sounds totally soul-sucking, but it's not all bad."

"The office life, I understand completely," I replied.

We fell into a semi-awkward quiet stretch after that.

She took another sip of wine. "So...tell me something fun. Like a weird hobby or a party trick."

I searched my brain. Blank. "I build furniture sometimes," I offered. "Just for the hell of it."

I was totally full of it. I built a side table once, and it fell apart in about two days. I just couldn't think of anything else off the top of my head.

Her brows lifted. "That's actually kind of hot."

I gave a polite laugh and looked down at my plate. I didn't know what to say to that. I wasn't trying to be hot. I wasn't trying to be anything, really. Just present, and that was hard enough.

Sara leaned forward slightly. "Okay, but...is there a catch? You're good-looking, smart, you can build stuff...so what's the tragic flaw?"

I looked up then, almost dropping my fork on my plate, when Keira's face suddenly popped into my head.

Every time. Right on cue.

"Well, I tend to get stuck in my own thoughts," I said finally. "I have a problem with overthinking things."

It was the truest thing I'd said all night. She smiled like she thought I was being charming.

"Well, I understand what that's like," she said, "but I usually just distract myself with sweets. You down for dessert?"

I smiled at that. "No thanks. I'm not really a sweets person."

She nodded and flagged the waitress anyway.

I pushed the last few bites of my meal around with my fork, half listening as she started talking about a trip she wanted to take to Vancouver. I knew I should engage more. Ask questions, offer something, anything.

But she wasn't the person I wanted to talk to, and there was no use in trying to pretend she was.

I watched her laugh at something I said as she tucked her hair behind her ear, swirling the wine in her glass. She was charming, no doubt. The kind of girl most people would be lucky to end up with.

But I wasn't most people.

The whole time, I kept thinking about how Keira would've made a face at the wine list, how she would've asked the bartender to just surprise her instead. How she'd take one bite of the cheese and say it tasted like a foot, then eat half of it anyway.

She had woven herself into every part of my life, and I saw her in everything. And maybe that was part of the problem.

After dinner, Sara leaned in a little. Her hand brushed mine, fingers light on my wrist.

"I had a good time," she said.

"Yeah," I replied quietly. "Me too."

She smiled. "Text me?"

"Sure," I lied.

We said goodbye outside, and I watched her walk toward the train station, her coat pulled tight and the wind catching her hair.

I slipped my hands into my pockets, turned in the other direction, and didn't look back.

***

I got home a little after seven. I dropped my keys in the bowl by the door, kicked off my shoes, and headed straight for the living room. I lay on the couch and turned on a show that I barely watched.

All I could think about was tonight and the way it had ended. I could tell that she wanted me to kiss her, but I just didn't have it in me. Not tonight.

After a while, I got up to turn off the TV and head to the bedroom when something made me pause.

The vintage lamp in the living room was still on. The soft, warm light cast a small circle on the couch. It sat in the same spot it always had, right where I put it when I moved in.

I hadn't really looked at it in a long time, not closely at least. I ended up replacing the wiring a few years back just to get it working again. But now, standing there in the quiet, I remembered the little details of it, the ones that mattered.

We found it at a flea market in Portland. She'd spotted it next to a pile of old books and vintage glassware. I thought it was hideous. She said it had character. So, of course, we got it.

The lamp ended up traveling everywhere with me over the years. I just couldn't seem to get rid of it.

I looked away, letting the memory pass.

After a beat, I finally turned off the lamp and made my way down the hall, dragging a little more than usual.

I brushed my teeth, rinsed my face with cold water, and caught a glimpse of myself in the mirror. My eyes looked tired, and my jaw was tight from where I held the stress of the day. This look had become my new norm.

I didn't bother turning on the overhead light in the bedroom. I just peeled off my shirt, grabbed a clean one, and climbed into bed.

The sheets were cold at first. I shifted around, trying to find a comfortable position, but nothing felt right.

After a while, I rolled onto my side and pulled the blanket up over my head the way I used to when I was a kid and couldn't fall asleep. The quiet pressed in from all sides.

A light rain started to tap against the window.

Usually, I found the sound calming. Something steady to fall asleep to.

But tonight, it didn't help.

***

THEN — AGE 21

PORTLAND, MAINE

The flea market was Keira's idea.

She'd read about it online and decided we needed a "day off from doing nothing," which, in her world, meant digging through crates of old books and pretending we had space in our place for antique furniture.

We were sharing a tiny two-bedroom apartment while we both finished school. Same city, different colleges. But it worked out for our living arrangement.

It was hot out that day. The kind of sticky heat that made you rethink being outside at all.

Keira had on this white sundress that hugged her body perfectly. It was one of the dresses she only ever wore on hot days. Her hair was up in a perfect ponytail tied with a yellow ribbon. She always looked beautiful to me, but that dress did me in.

She looked so happy, pointing at all the things that excited her, like a row of ceramic cherubs with bright red cheeks and a large, purely decorative, black porcelain cat from the 70s that served no purpose.

She knew she could always be herself around me, and it showed.

We wandered past a table of mismatched mugs and stopped in front of a stack of lamps.

Tall ones, short ones, cracked ones, lamps that probably hadn't worked in decades.

She picked up an oval-shaped one with a thick yellow and brown glass base and held it up as if she were appraising a diamond.

"This one," she said. "It looks like Pooh Bear's honey pot, don't you think?"

"I think it's ugly," I said, and she rolled her eyes.

"You have no taste, Miles."

I laughed. "I told you I'd let you pick the lamp, and you decided on the worst-looking one here."

"Taste is subjective." She smiled wildly. "And this one's coming home with us."

She carried it around to the seller like it were already her prized possession.

We paid ten bucks for it. I still, to this day, think we overpaid. The cord was worn, and the bulb flickered when we tested it, but she just smiled and said that made it better.

"It has character," she told me.

And when I saw her smile, I realized that was enough. If it made her happy, I could live with it.

She had put it on the side table in the living room when we got home.

Every night it glowed this soft, warm gold while she sat underneath it in her "comfy chair," as she called it, rereading *Pride and Prejudice* for at least the hundredth time since I'd known her.

When it stopped working six months later, she was devastated, and together we decided to never throw it away.

We pinky swore it, and in those days, a pinky swear was unbreakable.

Chapter 3

KEIRA

PRESENT DAY

Dylan liked to call Sundays our reset day. He'd wash the sheets, water the plants, and make something elaborate for breakfast while his favorite jazz album played in the background like we were in a movie about a couple who definitely had it all figured out.

I have to admit, despite the jazz, I did love watching him get excited about our Sundays together.

He stood at the kitchen counter pouring freshly ground coffee into the French press, humming a soft melody. The smell of toast filled our small apartment, mingling with lemon dish soap and laundry detergent.

This was our quiet life, bottled up with familiar scents and the comforts of home.

"Did you want honey or maple butter on your toast, babe?" he asked, already reaching for both.

"Honey, please," I said, slipping onto one of the barstools and pulling my sleeves over my hands.

He handed me a plate, perfectly balanced with eggs, sourdough, and fresh strawberries.

"Presentation is half the experience," he said with a grin, sliding his own plate across the counter before sitting beside me.

It was easy with Dylan. The kind of ease that didn't require too much effort.

We ate in silence for a while, the occasional clink of a fork or sip of coffee between us. He scrolled through an article about transit-oriented development, then turned his screen toward me.

"This new city project is implementing green corridors that connect neighborhoods to bike-friendly retail zones. I think I can pitch something like this to the Rockport Planning Board. On a much smaller scale, of course."

I smiled at that. I just loved watching the way his eyes lit up when he talked about his work. Dylan genuinely cared. He didn't try to impress anyone. He was present and dependable in a way that felt rare nowadays.

"You'll make it happen," I said, meaning it.

He leaned over and kissed my cheek. "You always say that."

He was right, I did. I said it because I believed in him. But sometimes, when he kissed me, I felt like I was watching it from outside my own body. Like I was playing the role of someone I was supposed to be, instead of someone I was.

I finished my coffee and smiled again, trying to shake the thought.

I usually closed the shop on Sundays during the winter because there wasn't enough foot traffic, but that day, I went in anyway. I told Dylan I needed to get some inventory work done before Monday, and he nodded like he always did in his own supportive way.

The truth was, I just wanted to be alone. I had a lot going on mentally, and I needed a minute to breathe. There was something about the shop when it was empty. No background chatter. No music. Just shelves and silence. It was my favorite kind of quiet.

I made some hot chocolate, the simple kind from the box, and lit my patchouli incense that sat right on my desk. Today was particularly cold, so I turned the heat up a bit.

Eventually, I sat on the floor behind the counter with a notebook in my lap and no idea what to write.

The third book just wasn't happening.

It wasn't that I didn't want to write it. I just couldn't bring myself to care about two people I barely believed in. They felt flat. Manufactured. Like I was writing what I thought love was supposed to look like instead of what I knew it really was.

And I knew.

God, I knew.

I used to dream about this exact life.

Owning a little bookshop by the coast, writing novels with a cup of tea going cold beside me. A quiet place with worn floorboards and a bell above the door. A life built around stories. Mine and everyone else's.

And somehow, I made it happen.

The shop was small but cozy. Locals knew me by name. Tourists came in off the harbor during the busy season, asking for beach reads and rainy-day romances.

I kept the windows clean and the front table fresh with new reads. I even had a small stand set up for me, the in-house author, and the two novels I had written. I'd curated everything myself.

It really had been perfect, but somewhere along the line, it started to feel like something was missing.

When I wasn't managing inventory or fixing the website, I wrote. I wrote every day, at least a page. Three years before, my debut romance took off in a way I'd never expected. It was soft and character-driven— two people and a fine-arts-museum-style meet-cute. It wasn't flashy, but it was relatable. It romanticized the perfect love in the best way.

I still got emails about it sometimes from readers who said it made them cry on a plane or stay up all night.

That book mattered. The second one, which had been a similar style romance, did too, in its own way.

But this third one?

This one kept coming up blank.

I stared at the open notebook in my lap, the same sentence scratched out and rewritten four times. I leaned my head back against the counter, eyes drifting to the ceiling fan turning slow and steady above me.

I had everything I'd ever wanted.

A shop. A career. A partner who loved me.

So why did it still feel like something was missing? What else could I possibly need?

***

The hours passed, and by two o'clock, the light had shifted.

Sun peeked through the windows in long, golden stripes, stretching across the wooden floorboards and catching in the corners of the shop I hadn't dusted in a few days.

Then, toward the end of the day, the clouds were back, and snow started to fall in heavy flakes. I was dealing with a bad case of writer's block, flipping aimlessly through books I already knew by heart.

Eventually, I gave up on drafting.

I flipped the lights off, gathered my things, and locked up the shop. I turned the corner toward the stairs and headed back up to my apartment, being extra careful not to slip on the slush.

Living upstairs from the shop couldn't have been better. No commute, no traffic, just twelve wooden steps and a door that stuck when it rained.

When I reached the top, I could hear Dylan in the kitchen. A small smile spread across my face as I stood just outside listening. The smooth sound played low from the speaker, and I could instantly tell it was his cooking playlist.

I opened the door and stepped inside.

He was standing at the stove, barefoot, stirring something that smelled like garlic and lemon. His hair was still damp from a shower and pushed back in that easy, effortless way he always wore it. Dirty blond, cut on the shorter side, but just long enough on top to stay a little messy without looking like he tried too hard.

He had that polished, all-American kind of look. Tall, broad shoulders, clean shaven, with warm hazel eyes that made people instinctively trust him. They always said he looked like someone you'd see in an upscale fashion catalog, and honestly, they weren't wrong. He was a total heartthrob.

Lola lay curled on the rug, tail thumping when she saw me.

"Hey, babe," he said, glancing over his shoulder. "You get some work done?"

"Sort of." I set my bag down by the door. "Mostly rearranged shelves and stared at my notebook."

He smiled. "Creative process."

"Something like that."

He turned back to the pan. "You want a glass of wine?"

"I would absolutely love a glass of wine." The thought of unwinding with a glass made me feel a little better.

I crossed the room and leaned on the counter, watching him for a minute.

These were the kind of moments I loved. The quiet, simple moments where we just existed perfectly in each other's space.

"So, how was your day?" I asked

"Oh, you know, the usual. Got a lot done and we've got fresh sheets on the bed." He gave me a small side smile, and I caught one of his dimples peeking through.

He poured me a glass of red wine and handed it to me before plating the pasta. It smelled delicious. He always prepared our meals like he wanted to impress, even after three years. But I could never deny it, the man knew how to cook.

We sat at the small table by the window, the one that overlooked the harbor. Boats bobbed in the distance, blurred by the thick, falling flakes.

I took a few bites and melted into my chair. I was much hungrier than I thought. "This is so delicious. I really needed this," I gushed.

He smiled as he twirled his fork. "You'd say that even if it tasted awful."

"Well, yes, but that's because I love you."

He laughed and took a sip of wine. We ate in silence for a few minutes before he set his fork down and glanced up at me.

"You okay?" he asked.

I looked up. "Yeah, why?"

"You're quieter than usual."

"I've just been in my head all day." I sighed, leaning back into my chair. "The book's not working. I just don't know what to write about. And I've had a migraine all day that's refusing to go away."

He nodded slowly. "Still stuck?"

"Worse than stuck. It feels...off. Like it's not even my thoughts anymore."

Dylan leaned back in his chair, thoughtful. "You want to take a break from it for a while? Do something else? Recharge a little?"

"I don't think it's that kind of stuck," I said. "It's not burnout. It's like the story I'm trying to write doesn't want to be told. There's a block."

He didn't push. That was one of the things I appreciated most about Dylan. He never tried to fix things he didn't understand. He just listened supportively and gave me his input.

"I'm sure it'll come," he said after a moment. "It always does. And when you finally figure it out, it's going to be amazing. Just like the other two."

I smiled, grateful. But the truth sat quietly between us, unspoken. This time, I wasn't sure it would.

***

Dylan went to bed around eleven.

He kissed the top of my head, mumbled something about turning off the lights, and disappeared into the bedroom. I told him I'd be in soon, after I got a little reading in.

Lola sat cozy on the rug in the living room while I curled up in the armchair by the front window. I pulled a blanket over my legs and opened *Pride and Prejudice* to the dog-eared page I knew by heart.

It was the part where Elizabeth finds out the truth about Darcy. Not just about what he's done, but how he feels. Vulnerable, awkward, a little too proud, but honest. Finally.

I read it slowly. I always did.

There was something about them that got to me every time. Not because it was perfect, but because it wasn't. Because they had to grow. Because they saw each other clearly, flaws and all, and still chose love.

That was the kind of romance I wanted to write.

Not just the falling, but the choosing. The changing. The staying.

I smiled to myself and tucked the blanket closer around my legs.

Some stories were worth rereading, even when you knew exactly how they ended.

***

THEN — AGE 16

CAMP RUSHWOOD, SEBAGO, MAINE

We weren't supposed to be out past curfew, but Camp Rushwood had always been more about tradition than enforcement.

The counselors rarely checked cabins once the flashlights were off, and Miles had found a back trail the previous summer that cut through the woods and led straight to the old firepit behind the nature center.

We'd been coming here since we were twelve, and this was our last summer. Our final chance to break the rules that had never really felt like rules to begin with.

The fire pit was nothing special, just a circle of stones, a few old logs to sit on, and the faint scent of ash still lingering from the last secret campfire. But it was ours. Quiet and hidden.

The night air was warm, and the woods buzzed with crickets and the occasional low croak of a bullfrog by the lake.

Miles was lying flat on his back in the grass, arms folded behind his head, eyes on the sky. His long, dark hair was wavy and a little unruly, fanned out around him with bits of grass and leaves caught in it. He hadn't noticed, or maybe he had and just didn't care. That would be typical of him.

He always had that look, like he belonged outside more than in, like nothing could ever fully pin him down.

I sat cross-legged next to him on a log, playing with the unfinished friendship bracelet in my hands, letting the yarn slip between my fingers.

"That one's Orion, right?" he asked, pointing lazily upward.

I squinted. "Pretty sure that's a plane."

He huffed a quiet laugh. "Whatever. Still looks cool."

"Try again," I said, stretching out beside him. "There's Orion, right there. See the belt?"

He nodded without looking at me. "You know, you grow up thinking the night sky is going to be this magical, glittering thing, and instead it's like...five dots."

"You're just looking at it all wrong," I said, scooting closer and pointing toward the eastern edge of the treetops. "See that cluster? That's the Pleiades."

He turned his head slightly, following my hand. "You're such a nerd."

"I know. And you love it."

I could feel his eyes on me then.

"What?" I said, glancing over at him

He shook his head. "Nothing."

Even in the low light, his eyes stood out. They were a clear, vivid blue, deep and always unreadable, like they saw more than he let on. They were the most beautiful eyes I had ever seen.

We went quiet after that. The night stretched around us, the quiet broken only by the rustling of the trees overhead and the distant sound of water lapping against the dock.

Then he cleared his throat and turned away from me. "So, uh— are you going to the dance thing?"

I raised an eyebrow. "You mean the end of camp formal?"

"Yeah. That."

"Why? You looking for someone to teach you how to dance?"

He let out a breath, like he was already regretting asking. "No, I just—I mean, I figured maybe…we could go. Together. You know, as friends."

I looked at him. He wasn't blushing exactly, but he was definitely avoiding eye contact.

"Miles Bennet, are you asking me to the dance?"

"I'm trying to," he said, clearly embarrassed.

A slow grin spread across my face. "Okay."

He blinked. "Okay?"

"Yeah," I said. "I'll go with you."

"Oh." He paused. "Cool."

"Good," I said, nudging his foot with mine.

He laughed, and I think that was the moment I knew.

I didn't dare say it out loud.

But I knew.

Chapter 4

KEIRA

PRESENT DAY

I was halfway through sorting the weekly invoices when my phone lit up with Maya's name.

My agent didn't usually call me on Mondays, and emails were more her style, so I wiped the ink from my fingers with the corner of my sleeve and picked up on the second ring.

"Hey Maya," I said. "Everything okay?"

"I've got good news," she said without preamble. "Are you sitting down?"

"Uhm—sort of. I'm hunched over a stack of shipping forms at the moment. Can that count?"

"Close enough." I could hear her smile through the line. "I've been working on something behind the scenes, and we finally got some bites."

I leaned back in the chair, intrigued. "Bites? What kind of bites?"

"Book tour bites. Indie bookstores, local events, and a few

regional chains. Nothing huge, just a handful of dates, but it'll be personal. The kind of thing your readers love."

My stomach fluttered. I hadn't been on a tour since the first book came out, and even then, it was just a handful of events at cozy coffee shops and coastal bookstores. I liked it that way, and she was right, my readers did too.

"What cities?" I asked, pretending I wasn't already anxious.

"Portland, obviously. Boston. New York. Seattle. Philadelphia. Chicago. Maybe San Francisco, if we can swing the timing. It's going to cut into Christmas, so I hope you don't mind celebrating the holiday on the road."

I nodded before I could stop myself, already reaching for a pen. "No, I don't mind. That shouldn't be a problem."

She ran through a few tentative dates and said she'd email me everything in a clean PDF. I told her thank you and hung up.

I sat back at my desk and circled the word "Chicago" at least ten times in black ink. I hadn't even realized I was doing it until I heard the front door creak open.

Jess stepped inside, clutching a hot coffee in one gloved hand and a paper bag in the other. Her cheeks were flushed pink from the cold, and snow clung to the hem of her long, olive-green coat. Her dark curls spilled out messily from under a knit beanie, and her scarf was wrapped so high it nearly covered up her septum piercing.

She had that constantly moving energy about her with quick steps, expressive green eyes, and a warm kind of chaos that never quite settled but somehow made everything around her feel more alive.

"I brought carbs," she said by way of greeting. "Goddamn, it's freezing out. Beth kicked me out of bed early to grab her some sustenance, and I had a feeling you might have needed a warm croissant this morning."

"I always need a croissant," I said, smiling.

She slid the bag across the desk and settled into the chair opposite me, tucking her legs beneath her, getting comfortable.

"How's the book coming along?" she asked, unwrapping her own pastry.

It was getting to the point where I couldn't take hearing that question anymore. I mean, how many more times could I answer without sounding completely irritated?

"Questionable," I said simply.

"Mm. The creative spirit lives."

I laughed under my breath. Jess had a way of saying things like that, dry and light-hearted, but never dismissive. She was the only person who could joke about my writer's block without making me feel like a total and complete failure.

We met when I first moved to Rockport. She's a townie, born and raised, with a sharp wit and an even sharper sense for good literature. We hit it off instantly and bonded over our shared love for the Brontë sisters and the quiet charm of old bookstores.

I hired her on the spot, not even sure what role I needed her for yet, just knowing I didn't want to run the shop without her.

Over time, she became more than an employee. She was my assistant, my sounding board, my daily dose of chaos and calm all rolled into one. We bickered like sisters and finished each other's sentences, and somehow, she kept both me and the bookshop running.

Truthfully, I didn't know what I'd do without her.

"So, I got a call from Maya this morning," I said.

Jess perked up. "Ooh. I'm sensing good news."

"You could say that. She wants to set up a small tour to prepare for the third book. It's mostly local stops—Boston, New York, a couple spots on the West Coast." I took a sip of my coffee and waited before adding, "And Chicago."

Jess didn't press right away. She just sipped her coffee and looked at me over the rim of the cup.

"And does *he* still live there?" she asked eventually, careful.

"I think so," I said. "I don't know, actually."

"Are you...okay with going?"

I scoffed. "Yeah. I mean, there are millions of people in Chicago. And besides, it's been years. The odds of us even running into each other are slim to none. He probably doesn't even live there anymore." I wanted that to make me feel better, but it didn't.

She didn't say anything for a moment. Then, said softly, "It's allowed, you know. To want to go for your book and be curious. Those two things can coincide just fine. And you know I'd never judge you. But Dylan is a good guy. Remember that. Don't do anything to him you wouldn't want someone to do to you."

I gave her a grateful look. "You're getting wise in your old age."

"Thank you. I'll be adding that to my resume: pastry courier and reluctant oracle."

Jess crumpled the empty paper bag and tossed it into the small bin by the counter. "Okay. I just wanted to stop in quick. If I don't get these pastries to Beth, she's going to lock me out again."

Beth and Jess were like oil and water, completely different in every way. But when they worked, it was something beautiful. I had never seen two people love each other quite like that.

"Tell the queen bee I said hi, would ya?"

"Of course." She stood and stretched, pulling her sleeves down over her hands. "You gonna be okay?"

"Yeah," I said, half smiling. "I've got a few hours before I need to do anything that requires any real brain function."

Jess hovered for a second like she wanted to say something else, then just nodded.

"Alright. Text me later? And work on that book, girl!"

"Will do."

The door chimed softly as she left, and then it was just me again. The shop stilled in her absence.

I closed up shop at the usual time. Snow still fell from the night before and frosted the windows.

I swept the floor, wiped down the counter, and turned the sign in the window to "Closed" with the same quiet rhythm I did every night. The bell above the door jingled as I locked up, the sound fading into the quiet of the empty street.

By the time I reached the top of the stairs to our apartment, the sky had already gone dark. The streetlights cast a soft glow over the sidewalk below, and the windows across the way were lit, warm against the night.

I kicked off my shoes in the hallway and set my keys in the small ceramic dish by the door, the one Dylan's sister had given us as a housewarming gift two years ago.

He had texted earlier—*Meeting ran long. I got you a fresh box of chamomile, it's in the cabinet. I love you.*

I reheated the pasta from the night before and poured myself a glass of red wine. I couldn't remember exactly when it had become my nightly ritual, but it was my version of self-care.

I stood at the sink while I ate, watching the boats bob on the water through the window above the faucet. The sounds of the neighborhood drifted up from the street below: muffled laughter and the distant thrum of a car stereo.

It was strange, sometimes, how a life could look so complete from the outside. How you could build something brick by brick and still feel like you were looking at your life from afar.

I hadn't realized how exhausted I was from the day, so I cleaned the dishes, wiped down the counter, and turned off the overhead light before moving into the bathroom. I started the shower and let the steam fill the room.

As I was getting undressed, I caught my reflection in the mirror and studied it for a moment. I didn't look all that different. Just a little older. A little more tired. But still me.

After my shower, I made my way into the living room, and I lit my favorite candle on the coffee table. I watched as it flickered gently, casting shadows up the wall in slow, thoughtful shapes.

I curled into the corner of the couch with my favorite wool blanket around my shoulders and my legs tucked beneath me. The windows were cracked just enough to let in a cold but refreshing breeze.

I had stacked some books beside me earlier. Some new releases I'd meant to preview for the shop, as well as some of my old favorites. I glanced at the pile, and instead reached for the notebook I kept in a book organizer by the coffee table. It was the one I didn't use for outlines or edits.

The cover was soft with wear, the pages marked with half-formed thoughts. I held it in my lap, letting my fingers rest on the cover for a moment.

And then I opened to a blank page.

The pen felt foreign in my hand at first. I stared at the paper for a long while, letting the quiet settle around me, letting the weight of the day loosen its grip. I thought about the book I was supposed to be writing. About Maya's tour schedule. About Chicago.

My pen hovered for a long time before it finally touched the page.

I didn't write a title.

No chapter heading. No clever opening line.

Just a sentence.

"Some people leave, and you still feel them everywhere."

I stared at it for a long time before shutting the book and turning out the light.

***

THEN — AGE 16

CAMP RUSHWOOD, SEBAGO, MAINE

The sky was still streaked with faint stars when we slipped away from the lodge.

I kicked off my shoes the second we hit the path, holding my glittery flats in one hand and trying not to trip on the uneven trail in my dress.

Miles walked beside me, hands in his pockets, tie undone, jacket long gone. The back of his shirt was damp from where he'd danced too hard, too long, with too many people.

We didn't say much as we walked down the long trail through the trees.

The lake came into view slowly, silver and soft in the moonlight. The boats were all docked. The canoes turned upside down.

Someone had left a hoodie balled up on the bench by the edge of the dock, but otherwise, it was just us.

We sat down, legs dangling over the side. I pulled the bracelet tighter on my wrist. It was the one we'd made that summer, knots uneven, colors slightly clashing. His matched mine.

"I'm not ready to go home," I said after a while.

Miles looked out over the water. "Yeah. Me either."

"You think next summer will be different?"

He shrugged, but not in a careless way. "Probably. But at least we'll be able to drive each other around instead of taking the bus."

I smiled and quietly agreed. He did have a point.

There was something about that night, about the way the air felt colder than it had in weeks, or the fact that we were sitting just close enough to feel the current between us, that made everything feel like it was slipping into something we couldn't have possibly been ready for.

He'd always just been my best friend. The person I could turn to for anything. The one I could tell my awful jokes to and still have him laugh like it was the funniest thing in the world.

So why did I suddenly get butterflies as his shoulder grazed mine?

I turned toward him, my heart pounding in my throat. "Did you mean what you said earlier? About the pact?"

He glanced at me, then nodded, a smile stretching across his face. "Yeah. I did."

I tried to laugh, but it came out too soft to sound casual. "Okay. So, if we aren't married by the time we're thirty, you'll settle for me."

We both laughed as he leaned his shoulder into mine, shoving me gently. "You really think we'll still know each other by then?"

"Why wouldn't we?" I said.

I looked at him then. The moonlight caught in his eyes. They'd always been my favorite thing about him, the way they shone when he was deep in thought, like now, staring out over the lake.

His dark hair had grown out longer than he usually kept it, curling slightly at the ends. It suited him. Effortless, and a little unruly. His nose was pink from too much sun earlier in the day, and there was a faint dusting of glitter on his sleeve from my corsage, like I had left my mark on him.

There was a large, flat rock just beside the dock, half-buried in the sand. I stepped onto it without thinking, the rough stone cool beneath my bare feet. It brought me just close enough to his height.

"I'm always going to be shorter than you," I whispered.

Miles walked up to me and smiled. "Not by much." He leaned in first. Just a little.

I hesitated before meeting him halfway.

The kiss was slow and a little unsure, but warm. His hand touched the side of my face for only a second, and when we pulled apart, I didn't say anything.

Neither did he.

We just stood there, our hands laced together, until someone down the hill started shouting curfew, and the spell finally broke.

Chapter 5

MILES

PRESENT DAY

I kicked off my shoes and tossed my keys onto the kitchen counter. The apartment was cold, but I didn't bother turning the heat up.

Work had run late, again. The firm had taken on a new tower proposal for the South Loop, and everyone was scrambling to pitch their vision to try and seal the deal with the boss.

I didn't scramble the way they did. I presented what I'd drawn, kept my answers tight, and left when the meeting ended. That was the difference between me and the rest of them. I didn't need to prove anything. I just needed the work to be good. And it always was.

I poured a glass of water and leaned against the counter, staring out across the living room at the view of the skyline. I was thinking about my plans for tomorrow. I had to head to Milwaukee for work, and was honestly looking forward to getting out of Chicago, even if it was just for a day trip.

The floor was cold beneath my feet as I moved through the

apartment, each step echoing in the quiet. I decided against music tonight. I wasn't really in the mood for any background noise.

Just then, my phone started to vibrate on the kitchen counter. I glanced at the screen and saw Mom lighting it up.

Shit. I'd been avoiding calling her the last few days. Not for any real reason. I just wasn't in a talk-about-your-feelings-with-Mom kind of mood. But she was relentless.

I let it ring a couple of times and finally hit accept. "Hey, Mom."

"Sweetheart, are you doing okay? I've been worried," she said, her voice already tight with panic.

"Yeah, Mom, I'm fine. Sorry. Work's just been… a lot lately."

She was a sweet woman. Too sweet sometimes. Always putting everyone else before herself. Hosting every holiday party, volunteering at every charity event, and practically living at the soup kitchen this time of year.

If Santa had a New England cousin, it was her.

"Miles, you'll never guess who I ran into the other day. Keira's mom!" My heart stopped. She kept talking. "Oh, I haven't seen her in ages. Apparently, Keira moved down to Rockport a few years ago, and she's doing well for herself there."

"That's great." The words scraped out of me. Hearing her name out loud hit something deep and sharp, and my stomach flipped.

"Hey, Mom," I said quickly, before she could keep going. "Do you think I can call you back later? I was just about to jump in the shower." It was a lie, but she didn't question it.

"That's fine, dear, I've got to fix up supper anyway. I love you!"

"Love you too," I said, and hung up.

God, you're such a coward.

I was glad she was doing well. I really was. But hearing anything about her felt like tearing open a part of me I kept stitched shut.

I went to the window, glass in hand, and looked out at the city.

The Hancock tower blinked in the distance, a quiet pulse in the dark. There was something strange about living among so many people and still feeling separate from all of it. But I'd gotten used to it. Liked it, even. The freedom in solitude.

Below, cars slid through intersections, honking their horns at each other as they passed. A man walked his dog across the street. A delivery guy propped open a door with his foot and disappeared inside.

Small lives in motion. All of them moving forward.

I stood there for a long time, fighting off whatever that call stirred up. I didn't want to feel it.

I didn't want to feel anything.

I turned off the kitchen lights and headed down the hallway toward my bedroom. Tomorrow was going to be a long day, and I'd regret it if I didn't call it a night now.

***

This wasn't the first time I'd taken the train to Milwaukee. I made the trip every few weeks for a residential build we were finishing up outside the city.

Most of the guys on the team drove, including me, but I didn't mind the train. I liked the stillness of it, the way it gave me permission to do nothing for a couple of hours. No emails, no small talk, no calendar alerts buzzing at the worst time. Just straight motion and space to think.

There was a record shop that I wandered into sometimes when I was in the area. The kind with worn hardwood floors, alphabetized bins, and handwritten labels that said things like "Better than you remember" or "Beat up the Beat."

I stopped at a corner café on my way there, one of those quiet places with fogged-up windows and a handwritten menu taped to the glass. The kind of spot that smelled like fresh espresso and burnt sugar.

I ordered a black coffee and a bagel with cream cheese, nodded politely to the barista, then found a seat by the window while I waited.

The place was a little cramped, but it felt good to slow down for a minute.

Outside, the sidewalk was wet from snowy slush as people sloshed through, making their way to work.

When my order was ready, I thanked them and headed back out into the cold; hands full, breath clouding in the air, and the record shop just a few blocks ahead.

The guy behind the counter nodded when I walked in but didn't speak. That's what I liked about this place. No small talk. Just the sound of an old LP playing on the overhead speakers. It was some punk record I've never heard of.

I took my time flipping through the rows.

They had a little bit of everything: some electronic, a little classic rock, and a section labeled Late 90s/Early 2000s Revival that made me feel both old and oddly comforted. I thumbed past a dusty copy of Radiohead's *Kid A*, a scratched-up *No Strings Attached* by *NSYNC, and a mint-condition *The Miseducation of Lauryn Hill*. That one made me pause. My mom used to play it on weekend mornings while cleaning the house, singing along under her breath with a dish towel slung over her shoulder.

Funny how music sticks with you like that.

Further down the row, I found The Strokes, Blink-182, and even a copy of Dido's *No Angel*, which I hadn't thought about in over a decade but somehow still knew all the lyrics to.

I wasn't really looking for anything specific, just letting the familiarity of it all wash over me. I was surrounded by old covers, forgotten names, and pieces of time I didn't realize I'd packed away.

I stopped when I hit a Coldplay album. *Parachutes*. A special yellow pressing in matte.

My hand froze when I saw it, then slowly, almost automatically, I pulled it out from the bin. The sleeve was worn. Probably played a hundred times before ending up here. I turned it over in my hands, reading the track list on the back without really seeing it. I already knew what was there. First track, second side. "Yellow."

That used to be our song.

And just like that, she was everywhere again.

***

THEN — AGE 17

PORTLAND, MAINE

I had been sitting at home, enjoying my Friday night after a long week of school and pointless homework, when I got a text from Keira around 6 p.m.

She'd had a rough day and was waiting for me to let her in.

I don't really remember the details, but I think one of her teachers had shredded her short story, or maybe it was the workshop group that picked it apart too fast.

Either way, she came downstairs to my room, dropped her bag on the couch, and collapsed right beside it.

I was curled up on my bed, eating leftover Chinese food from the night before. We had this hole-in-the-wall all-you-can-eat place we loved, and I always snuck some leftovers home, even though you technically weren't supposed to. Keira always got so mad at me for doing it, but she'd be thanking me when she came over the next day. Every time.

She lay there on the couch, one arm flung over her eyes like the weight of everything had gotten too loud.

I handed her the rest of my plate without asking. She sat up halfway and took it without looking at me, but her leg bumped mine as I sat down next to her, and she didn't move it away.

"You wanna talk about it?"

"Ugh, later." She said, her voice dripping with drama.

We ate on the couch, legs touching, the TV low in the

background playing one of our favorite shows that we must have watched at least a hundred times. She started quoting it halfway through, mumbling lines around bites of noodles like the words were muscle memory.

"You're such a dork," I said.

She smiled without looking at me. "Takes one to know one."

I studied her a bit longer before making a decision. "Come on, let's go."

"Go? Go where?" she said, surprised.

"For a drive so we can fix that shitty day you had."

A wide smile spread across her face as she jumped up and grabbed her coat. I used to drive us everywhere back then, anywhere she wanted to go.

She didn't have her license yet. Her excuse was that she was scared of failing the road test, even though she was probably better behind the wheel than I was.

So I drove. Every time. And it never mattered once where we were going.

It had started snowing as we got closer to the water, the kind of soft, slow flakes that didn't really stick, just floated around like they had nowhere to be. Just like us.

We drove along the coast, windows fogged at the corners, streetlights casting long, golden beams onto the wet road. The ocean was just beyond the guardrail, black and endless. She rolled her window down halfway just to breathe it in.

"Mmmm. It smells like salt and pine trees," she said. "And fireplaces. You smell that?"

I nodded, feeling a smile forming that I couldn't help. "Yeah, I do."

Keira sat back, twisting toward me in her seat and sipping on her hot chocolate. She was wearing a navy blue peacoat with a scarf wrapped around her neck, her cheeks flushed pink from the cold.

"I love that smell so much," she murmured. "It smells like Christmas, you know?"

47

I smiled wide and laughed quietly to myself. She always said stuff like that. Stuff that made no sense and all the sense at the exact same time. I loved that about her.

A few minutes later, I pulled into an empty beach lot without thinking.

The whole place was deserted except for the wet asphalt under the tires, a few wooden picnic tables, and the faint sound of waves crashing somewhere beyond the dunes. The headlights stretched out into the dark.

Keira raised an eyebrow. "What are we doing?"

"Nothing," I said, cutting the engine. "Just stopping for a bit."

She watched me, skeptical but amused, then leaned her head back against the seat and sighed. "Okay, but if this turns into a horror movie situation, I'm leaving you behind." I laughed under my breath and turned the key one notch to keep the music on.

My old iPod was still plugged into the aux cord with the shuffle mode going.

And then, as if it was meant to be, "Yellow" started to play.

The opening notes hit the speakers low and steady, and something in the air shifted.

Keira turned toward me slowly, eyes narrowing, not because she was annoyed, but because she knew. She knew what that song was, what it meant to both of us, even if neither of us had said it out loud before.

They played it as the night was winding down, the last slow song at the end of the summer formal. Our last night at Camp Rushwood. It was the first time I'd asked her to dance. It was the night everything changed between us.

I reached for the volume and turned it up. Not too loud. Just enough to feel it in the air.

Then I got out and walked around to her side, opening her door like we were somewhere fancier than a beach parking lot with slushy tire tracks and snow in the sand.

"You're not serious," she said, half laughing.

"Come on."

"It's freezing."

"I'll keep you warm."

She squinted up at me, lips twitching like she was trying not to smile too wide. "That's your line?"

"I've got better ones," I said. "But they'd sound stupid right now."

She hesitated.

"Come on," I said, nonchalantly, and then reached for her hand.

We walked out into the lot, the snow falling quiet around us. She tucked her coat tighter around herself, shivering as she stepped closer.

I slipped one arm around her waist, the other holding her hand. Her gloved fingers curled inside mine, and she looked up at me with that expression she always got when she didn't want to admit she was feeling something big.

The music played on.

We didn't really dance; we just moved slowly together. Her head rested against my chest, and my chin dipped toward her hair. She was right, the air did smell amazing, but there was nothing better than the smell of her vanilla honey shampoo that lingered on her hair.

Her breath warmed the space between us, rising in soft little clouds that disappeared as fast as they came.

She looked up at me, her eyes flicking down to my mouth for half a second. I hadn't kissed her since the last night at camp. We hadn't even talked about it since. But I knew if I didn't kiss her now, I'd regret it for the rest of my life.

So I did.

It wasn't rushed or clumsy, but it wasn't perfect, either. Our noses bumped, and we both smiled a little, but once we got our groove, it turned into the kind of kiss that made everything else fall away.

My hand slid up to the side of her face, thumb brushing her

cheekbone, and she leaned into it like she'd been waiting for it all night.

When we pulled back, barely an inch between us, she didn't say anything right away.

Then, softly, with her eyes still closed, she said, "It's about time."

I laughed, because yeah, it kind of was. And we both knew it. And maybe we didn't know what we were yet, or what would happen next, but that moment?

It was enough.

***

PRESENT DAY

The song ended, and for a moment, the lights in the record store felt too bright.

The overhead lights buzzed faintly. I held the record in my hand, unable to put it down. I slipped it back into its sleeve, careful not to bend the corners, and carried it with me to the front.

I didn't need it. I could stream the whole thing in two seconds from my phone. But that wasn't the point.

"Good choice," the girl behind the register said, ringing it up. "That album holds up."

I nodded, but didn't say anything.

I finished up my work for the day and was ready to head back. The train home hummed beneath me, steady and slow, cutting its way through a snow-laced landscape that blurred past the window in gray streaks and leafless trees.

Milwaukee was already fading behind me, the last of its rust-colored brick buildings slipping into the horizon.

The sky was heavy with clouds, thick and low like they were pressing down on the whole Midwest. I leaned back against the seat, coat unzipped, the Coldplay record resting flat across my lap in a paper bag.

It had been years since I'd listened to the whole album all the way through. I didn't need to since I already had it memorized front to back. Not just the music, but everything it carried.

The weight of it. The way that listening to it always took me somewhere else.

The car was quiet with just the low rumble of the train and the occasional crinkle of snack wrappers a few rows up.

I closed my eyes and rested my head against the seat.

I wasn't sleeping well. I'd been waking up at three a.m. most nights for no good reason, lying there in the dark with the city lights creeping under the blinds. Sometimes I'd scroll through my phone. Sometimes I'd read. Sometimes I'd just stare at the ceiling like it had all the answers.

My thirties were around the corner. Most of my friends were married now, with some already starting families. They were buying homes, settling down. It was like watching a picture-perfect movie unfold, everyone moving toward their happy ending while I was still trying to figure out what mine looked like.

It wasn't that I didn't want something like that. I just didn't know how to want it anymore.

Somewhere, there was a version of myself I carried quietly, tucked under the surface, that no one else got to see. And maybe that version still hadn't found its way back to me. Maybe that version still belonged to someone else.

I let out a slow breath and looked down at the record again. I took it out of the paper bag and stared at the cover. I could see my reflection faintly in the plastic. My eyes were tired with dark circles rimming them.

I noticed a small dent in the corner of the album sleeve. I ran my thumb over it, not trying to fix it, just feeling its character. Wondering where it'd been, how many memories it held for someone else.

Looking at the record now made me remember her laugh and the way she could never quite eat an ice cream cone without dripping it all over her hand. I remembered how she hated tomatoes but loved tomato sauce. I remembered her voice in the middle of the night when we were fifteen, whispering across the landline, when the whole world was asleep except us. How she used to say my name when she was tired…soft and low, like she'd just pulled it out of a dream.

The train slowed as we pulled into the northern edge of the city. I sat up straighter, rubbing away the tired from my eyes, and glanced out the window. Snow had started to fall again, harder now, thick flakes swirling past the windows in sheets of silver and white.

Chicago looked gray and familiar as we approached, all steel and concrete under a dull winter sky.

It wasn't Portland. It never would be. But over the last five years, I'd stopped feeling like a visitor. I belonged here now. Or at least, I'd convinced myself I did.

As the train came to a stop, the doors hissed open. I stood with my coat draped over one arm and stepped off into the familiar noise and motion of the city.

Chapter 6

KEIRA

PRESENT DAY

We walked home from dinner, past shuttered shops and glowing porch lights, the cold air sharp against our cheeks.

Dylan's hand was wrapped in mine, comfortable and warm. The late afternoon air was crisp, and the streets along town were quieter than usual, except for a few locals walking with hot takeaway cups in gloved hands.

"I was thinking," he said, his breath visible in the cold, "we should do a dessert table instead of a traditional cake. Maybe mini pies and little pastries? Make it more of a you sort of vibe."

I smiled, because it was something I would've suggested if I'd had the energy to think about it. "That actually sounds perfect."

"And I emailed the venue this morning to confirm the tasting. They said we can bring Jess with us, too, if you want her opinion on the florals."

He always remembered the details. He was thoughtful that way, always thinking a few steps ahead, making sure things were handled, so I didn't have to stress too much since I already had so much on my plate.

"You don't think we're over planning?" I asked quietly. "Sometimes I wonder if we should just elope."

He looked over at me, amused. "You? Eloping? You'd regret not having your friends and family there. And Jess would literally disown you."

"True," I said, then added, "It's just a lot. All of it."

"I know," he said, gently. "But it's all going to be worth it. The only thing that matters is you and me. The rest is just noise."

I smiled at that, though something still bit at me.

We walked in silence after that. A few window displays were already decorated for the holidays with garlands, twinkle lights, and colorful ribbons. Everything looked soft and perfect.

"I actually have something to tell you," I said quietly.

He slowed. "Okay."

"Maya got me set up with a book tour to promote the fact that I'm writing a new one. I got the final schedule earlier today. I'll be leaving in a couple of weeks and hitting a bunch of major cities."

"Keira, that's amazing! I'm so happy for you," he said.

"The only downside is it's going to run through the holidays, so I won't be home for Christmas."

He didn't miss a beat. "Then I'll come to you," he said simply. "Wherever you are."

I looked up at him, surprised. "You'd really do that?"

"Of course I would," he said, gently squeezing my hand. "Keira, this is a huge moment for you. You've worked so hard for this. I want to be there cheering you on, not holding you back."

A lump formed in my throat, uninvited. He didn't guilt me. He didn't flinch. He just supported me. Like he always did.

"I don't know how I got so lucky," I said softly. "Sometimes I feel like I don't deserve you."

He smiled and stopped walking, turning to face me. "You didn't get lucky. We both chose each other. And continue to do so every day."

And standing there, in the middle of our sleepy little town with his hands wrapped around mine and the world quiet around us, I wanted to believe that was enough. That I could shove the second-guessing to the back of my mind. The least I could do was try.

It was just a bad case of cold feet. That's all it was.

***

3 WEEKS LATER

The climbing gym wasn't usually part of my routine, but Jess had a way of convincing me to say yes to things that were out of my comfort zone.

I'd spent the past week packing, coordinating last-minute book tour details, and answering wedding emails I'd been avoiding. My brain felt like a browser with too many tabs open. So when she texted and told me to meet her at Granite & Grit for a climb and a break from reality, I didn't hesitate.

Inside, it smelled faintly of chalk, sweat, and rubber mats, but somehow the space felt clean and open. Kids were scrambling up rope walls in the back while a few regulars I'd seen here before scaled the runs in the bouldering section. Indie music played overhead, and a heater near the entrance kept the space from being too cold. I pulled off my coat, rolled up my sleeves, and let Jess drag me toward the wall.

"You gonna stare at it all night or actually climb it?" she said, already clipping her wild hair up with a practiced twist.

I smiled and clapped some chalk into my palms. "Mentally preparing."

"You're stalling."

"Same thing," I muttered, tightening my grip on the chalk bag.

Jess crouched to re-velcro her shoe, her voice casual. "So. How's the wedding planning going?"

I groaned. "You already asked me this yesterday."

"What? I'm your maid of honor. It's in my job description to annoy you about it."

I pulled myself onto the first hold, stretching for the next one. "It's just been a lot lately."

"A lot...or too much?" she asked, not unkindly.

I hesitated. "I mean..." I paused halfway up the route, finding my footing. "Of course I want to get married."

"To Dylan?" Jess said it gently.

I made it to the top, touched the finish hold, then dropped down with a soft thud onto the mat.

"Yes, Jess. To Dylan," I said, brushing chalk off my leggings. "How could I not? We've been together forever, and that's just what you do."

Jess raised an eyebrow. "You don't sound very sure."

"I'm just tired," I said, avoiding her eyes. "Planning everything has been nonstop. The wedding is only a few months away, and I feel like I barely have enough time to prepare everything."

She nodded, then grabbed the wall herself, pulling up with her usual ease. "You used to talk about getting married like it was this beautiful, magical thing."

"I still think it is."

Jess made it halfway up before pausing to look down at me. "Then what's bothering you? Because I know it's not all the planning."

I hesitated, then said, "It's not Dylan. It's me."

She dropped down and landed lightly, hands on her hips. "Talk to me, Keira. This is what I'm here for."

"I don't know." I sat down on the edge of the mat. "It's like...I have everything I thought I wanted. He's wonderful. The bookstore's doing well. I have a ring, a dress and a date. But there's this little voice in the back of my head that keeps asking if I'm sure."

Jess sat beside me. "Are you?"

I looked at my hands. "I want to be."

"That's not the same thing."

I sighed. "It's just cold feet. Everyone gets cold feet."

"Cold feet feels different than whatever this is." Jess was quiet for a second. "Do you love him?"

I nodded. "Yes. But sometimes I wonder if I love him the way I'm supposed to. The way a wife would love a husband."

We sat there while someone nearby let out a loud whoop after finishing a difficult route.

Jess bumped her shoulder against mine. "There is no one right way to love someone, and you don't have to have it all figured out right now. But you do have to be honest. With him and with yourself."

"I know."

She grinned. "And until then, you can hang out here with me and pretend bouldering fixes everything."

I let out a laugh. "Thanks for dragging me here."

"Anytime. Now go climb again. That route was way too easy for you."

We stayed for another hour, climbing until my arms ached and my mind felt lighter than it had in days.

By the time I got home, the sun was already down, and the familiar quiet of the apartment wrapped around me like a blanket.

Later that night, I stood in my room, staring at the chaos on my bed. I was leaving in the morning and felt beyond overwhelmed.

I didn't mean to over-pack. I'd promised myself I'd travel light with just the essentials, but apparently, "essentials" meant three pairs of boots, six sweaters, five pairs of jeans, four dresses, and two handfuls of shirts. And that was just my clothing. I still had everything else to pack.

The suitcase sat open on the floor, already half full. I knelt beside it, folding a cream-colored turtleneck, tucking it neatly between my jeans and the toiletry bag I hadn't zipped yet. A stack of pre-signed bookplates sat next to me, along with the travel itinerary Jess had color-coded with tabs. I'd have to thank her for that one later.

Chicago was first.

I'd chosen it. Not because it made logistical sense. But because I wanted to get it over with. Maybe I just needed to prove to myself that I could go there and be fine.

I sat on the edge of the bed and looked down at my hand. The diamond from my engagement ring caught the light. It was beautiful and exactly what I wanted. Simple, classic. Everything it was supposed to be.

Dylan had proposed to me on the beach at sunset near where I grew up. There was nothing flashy about it. Just the two of us. Intimate, just like I always wanted.

I thought about my conversation with Jess and decided to leave my ring. I slid it off slowly, feeling the indent it left behind, and walked over to my dresser. I opened the top drawer and tucked it into a small velvet pouch, then pushed it gently to the back.

I didn't want to risk losing it, especially not while traveling. Not with hotel rooms and rushed schedules and plane rides. It felt safer to leave it at home.

I looked around the room. It was warm, cozy, and full of my things. The curtains were linen. The bookshelf was organized perfectly. There was a framed photo of Dylan and me from our trip to Bar Harbor last year on the dresser. We looked happy in it. Or at least our version of happy.

It all felt very... cookie-cutter.

I'd started to notice that some days, I felt like I was performing it. Going through the motions of someone who had everything she'd ever wanted, while a small voice in the back of my mind whispered: You used to feel more than this.

I shook off the discontentment and moved to the dresser to double-check that my spare charger was packed.

I was heading into one month of scheduled appearances, bookstore panels, tidy hotel rooms, and smiling across tables at people who read my work more intimately than anyone else in my life.

I loved this job. That was the part no one got to see—the way it felt to meet a reader who clutched your book like it had gotten them through something, or stayed up until two in the morning crying over a character you made up while you were cooking dinner one night. I had worked hard for this. It hadn't been handed to me.

The bookshop, the career, the growing mailing list, the podcast interviews—it was all earned. One late night, one blank page, one signature at a time.

Still, I wasn't naïve. The more successful I got, the more people wanted something from me. Stories. Opinions. Engagement. The pressure to stay relevant, especially as a woman writing about love, was heavier than anyone liked to admit.

I was proud of the work I did, but I was tired too. Tired of trying to be accessible and profound and relatable all at once. Tired of pretending I was still inspired when the truth was, I hadn't felt lit up by a story idea in months.

Dylan knocked on the frame of the door.

"You want tea before bed, babe?" he asked. "I was going to make some."

I turned with a smile. "Sure. Chamomile, please, with a little milk and honey."

He lingered for a moment in the doorway. "You sure you don't want me to drive you to the airport tomorrow?" he asked.

I shook my head without looking at him. "It's easier this way. I don't want to uproot your day. Besides, you have a client meeting that you can't miss, and I already booked the car."

He nodded as he turned to head toward the kitchen.

I folded one last sweater and pressed it flat before closing the suitcase.

I checked my phone. Jess had texted me an updated itinerary. My flight landed at Midway around 1:40 p.m. She'd already arranged a rideshare and had the boutique hotel I was staying in near the South Loop all good to go. I had a signing the following afternoon and a Q&A panel that evening.

I could do a couple of days in Chicago. It would be over before I even knew it, and then everything could get back to normal.

I slipped the phone back in my pocket and stepped out of the bedroom. Dylan was pouring water into mugs, humming quietly to himself. The kitchen lights gave the apartment a soft glow, and for a second, I stood there, watching him in our space.

This was my life. And it was good.

It didn't have to be perfect to be real.

But there was a difference between contentment and connection, and I was still figuring out where I fell between the two.

Later in bed, the room was quiet except for the soft rustle of sheets and the distant sound of the boats and buoys bobbing outside the window.

Dylan's hand traced along my arm, slow and gentle, like he was testing the mood. He pressed a kiss to my shoulder, his mouth warm against my skin. I brought my hand up to his face and kissed him back.

"You sure you're not too tired?" he asked, his voice low against my neck.

I gave him a small smile, "No. I'm okay."

He kissed me again, longer this time, his hand sliding under the hem of my shirt. I didn't stop him. My body responded the way it always had, with muscle memory, warmth, and ease. We'd been together long enough for this to feel natural.

But even in the closeness, I felt separate. Not because Dylan was doing anything wrong…he wasn't. He was gentle, respectful, loving in that quiet, consistent way that had made me fall for him in the first place. He asked. He waited. He never rushed me.

It wasn't him. It was me.

My thoughts refused to settle. They kept circling back to things that didn't belong, and underneath it all were feelings I couldn't shake.

I tried to refocus, to ground myself in the present—the way his thumb brushed over my hipbone, the way he whispered my name. But even then, a part of me felt like I was lying. Not to him, but to myself. Pretending I was all there when some essential part of me was miles away, deep in the back of my mind.

Dylan paused, eyes searching mine.

"You okay?" he asked softly.

I blinked, then nodded. "Yeah. Just distracted, I think. I'm sorry, babe, I guess I'm just a little nervous about the trip."

He studied me for a second longer before giving me a half smile, already pulling the blanket up over both of us. "No pressure," he said, brushing a kiss to my forehead. "Just try to get some sleep."

I didn't respond. I just moved closer, resting my head against his chest, letting the steady rhythm of his breathing fill the space between us. At least he cared enough to still try.

***

THEN — AGE 18

PORTLAND, MAINE

I don't remember who threw the party. Some college guy Miles knew, maybe. Some kid whose parents were out of town for the Fourth of July weekend and had a big house with too much alcohol and not enough common sense.

We had all just graduated and were looking for any excuse to celebrate our first summer as official adults.

I'd barely stepped into the backyard when I realized it was loud. The music blasted from floor speakers, girls danced barefoot, and red Solo cups littered the grass like confetti. The air smelled like beer and cheap weed.

Miles met me outside when I got there, grinning like a troublemaker. His dark hair was tucked under a backwards cap, and he looked effortlessly cool in that way he always did.

Without trying. Without even meaning to.

We stuck close to each other that night and drank more than we normally did. I remember laughing, leaning into his chest, pretending the butterflies in my stomach were from the music and general excitement and not the way his hand rested on my waist.

I felt the press of his fingertips at my hips, warm against the strip of skin where my shirt had ridden up. At some point, I'd moved closer without realizing it, and he noticed. His arm tightened around me, pulling me in just a little more.

"Easy there, Sullivan. Any closer and I might start thinking you're into me," he said, that familiar grin tugging at his mouth.

"Would that be such a bad thing?" The words slipped out before I could stop them.

They hit him the same way they hit me. His grin faded, and suddenly he was looking at me differently, blue eyes steady and searching, like he was trying to figure out if I meant it.

And then, without warning, someone yelled, "Cops!"

Everything exploded.

Kids scattered like ants. Someone knocked over a speaker. A girl dropped her phone and screamed. Miles grabbed my hand before I could panic and yanked me through the side yard.

"This way," he said, already running.

We jumped a fence, well, I tried to jump and nearly fell, but he caught me. We cut through two backyards, breathless and laughing. By the time we reached his street, my heart was pounding hard enough to hurt.

His house was only a few blocks away. We ducked behind his neighbor's hedge, caught our breath, and then he nodded toward his basement window.

"In," he said, crouching.

I blinked. "You want me to crawl through the window?"

He looked up at me, grinning. "Unless you wanna knock and explain to my mom why we're home at two a.m. Come on, Keira, you've snuck down here a hundred times."

"Yeah, well, I've hardly had to do it buzzed." I rolled my eyes but bent down anyway, slipping off my shoes before he helped me climb inside. I tumbled onto the carpet in the dark, giggling quietly as I straightened up.

"Smooth landing," he teased, climbing in after me and pulling the window shut behind him.

His room smelled like laundry detergent and the faint scent of cologne he always used too much of before school.

There were clothes on the floor, books stacked messily on his desk, and a Red Hot Chili Peppers poster curling off the wall. It was the most familiar place in the world, considering I basically lived here in my spare time. This house was my second family.

I stood there, trying to catch my breath, still laughing, the rush of it all clinging to my skin.

Then I turned to him.

"That was insane," I said.

"You loved it."

I shook my head, smiling. "You've always been a bad influence."

"Maybe." He stepped closer. "But you still follow me everywhere."

That stopped the air in my lungs. The room went quieter somehow, like the outside world had clicked off. We were standing close. Not on purpose, but close enough that I could feel the warmth of his breath on my cheek.

"You should probably change," he said after a second, voice softer now. "You've got grass stains everywhere."

I glanced down at my knees. "Shit, you're right." I laughed.

"I'll—uh—grab you something."

He turned toward his dresser and started digging through the drawers. I sat on the edge of his bed and pulled my hair down from its ponytail, my fingers trembling slightly even though I didn't know why. It wasn't like this was the first time I'd slept over.

He handed me an old t-shirt, one I'd worn before, from that trip to his cousin's lake house. I took it and turned toward the corner of the room so I could change comfortably.

When I turned back around, he was sitting on the floor, knees up, elbows resting on them like he didn't know what to do with himself.

"Sorry," he said, looking up at me. "This night turned into kind of a mess."

"I liked it."

He smiled a small crooked smile. "Yeah?"

I nodded, then sat beside him, close enough for our shoulders to touch.

And then he said, so quietly I almost missed it, "You know, you're my favorite person."

It didn't feel like a line. Not a moment of charm or timing. Just... the truth. And when I looked at him, I felt something bloom deep in my chest. Something inevitable.

He lifted his hand and swept a loose strand of hair back behind my ear. His fingertips lingered just long enough to graze my cheek. "Can I kiss you?" he asked.

I didn't answer. I just leaned in and met him halfway.

We stayed like that for a while, knees pressed together on the carpeted floor, trading soft kisses that kept deepening with every breath. I could feel the way his hand trembled slightly when it touched my hip.

He pulled back just enough to search my face, his thumb brushing along my cheekbone.

"We don't have to," he said. "Really, Keira. We can stop anytime."

I nodded, eyes not leaving his. "I know."

He waited another second, like he needed to be sure, like he wasn't going to move forward unless I really wanted it too.

"I want to," I said, quietly but clearly. "I want it to be you."

His breath hitched in his throat, and he nodded slowly. Then he kissed me again, and something in the air shifted.

We tumbled onto his bed, still in our clothes, laughing hard when I tried to kick off my jeans too fast and he knocked his head against the dresser. But there was this tenderness between us, an unspoken effort to be gentle. To pay attention. He asked if I was okay at every step, and every time I said yes, I meant it a little more.

When his shirt came off, I saw him blush. It made me smile. He wasn't trying to be smooth or confident. He was just him. My best friend. The boy I'd loved since we were kids.

By the time our clothes were gone and the blanket was pulled over us, the only light in the room came from the streetlamp outside the window, slanting gold across his wall.

He was quiet when he moved over me. Careful. I held his face in my hands and watched every shift in his expression.

It wasn't perfect, but it didn't need to be.

There was a second—right before—when we both froze, breathing hard, and I whispered, "Are you okay?"

He nodded, and when he looked down at me, there was something close to wonder in his eyes. "You're the only person I've ever been sure about." And then we weren't talking anymore.

It hurt a little. But not in the way I'd been afraid of. It felt like crossing a line we couldn't come back from, but neither of us wanted to anyway.

And then it was just us, tangled in quiet and the kind of closeness that stayed long after everything else faded. After, we lay there under the blanket for a while, my head on his chest, his heartbeat wild against my cheek.

Neither of us said anything for a long time.

But I remember thinking: This is it. This is how you know.

Because for the first time, the world outside that basement felt completely still. And nothing else mattered except the way his thumb moved across my back, over and over, like he didn't even realize he was doing it.

Like he was trying to memorize every detail of who I was right then. And I knew I would never forget the way it made me feel.

Chapter 7

KEIRA

PRESENT DAY

CHICAGO, ILLINOIS

The wheels hit the runway with a heavy jolt, hard enough to make my breath catch. The plane groaned beneath us, brakes shrieking, bodies lurching forward like we'd all forgotten gravity had a say in our arrival.

A moment later, the cabin was filled with the soft rustle of motion: seatbelts unclipping, phones switching back on, the quiet shuffle of people stretching, their limbs stiff from the flight.

Outside the window, the city stretched beneath a wintery sky the color of worn steel. The buildings rose tall and cold in the distance, their edges blurred with the quiet threat of snow. I'd seen Chicago in movies and on postcards, but I had never been here before.

Not until now.

The last time I saw Miles was the day he packed up and left Portland for this city. I didn't know then that it would be the last time. We'd said "see you later" like it meant something, like we believed it. But time had a way of pulling at even the strongest ties, unraveling them thread by thread. And somewhere along the way, Miles unraveled right out of my life.

I gripped the armrest loosely, heart fluttering in that strange, familiar way when you're anticipating something. But it wasn't the airport that made my stomach twist. It was the idea of this place. Of him, possibly, somewhere in it.

I shook my head and decided to try and keep my thoughts on work. That's why I was here. That's what was important. Not some fantasy of a life I once had. Or hadn't had.

I moved through the terminal slowly with the crowd, my boots clicking against the linoleum, the handle of my carry-on warm in my hand from how long I'd been holding it. I rolled it behind me as the stream of passengers funneled toward baggage claim, their faces drawn, headphones in, kids trailing behind parents like sleepy little shadows.

At carousel six, I stood with my arms crossed, the hum of the conveyor belt buzzing in my ears as I watched suitcase after suitcase come crawling around the corner. Black, navy, black again. A pink one with a scarf tied to the handle.

Mine showed up near the end, deep green and scuffed in the corners. It had seen its fair share of airports, connections, and missed flights.

I dragged it off with both hands and let it drop with a dull thud beside my carry-on. The ride share pickup zone was outside, across two crosswalks and beneath a concrete overhang that funneled the wind like a tunnel. My fingers went numb instantly, the uncomfortable cold sliding down the back of my neck.

They called this place the Windy City for a reason, and the winter chill was no joke. I zipped my coat all the way up and adjusted the strap on my bag. My phone vibrated—Darren in a black Toyota Camry is arriving now—and within a minute, I was tossing my luggage in the trunk and sliding into the back seat with a muffled, "Hi there."

The heat blasted from the vents. I didn't say much else and was grateful that my driver didn't either. I honestly have never been one for needing to fill the dead air with unnecessary small talk.

Chicago seemed deeper into winter than back on the East Coast. Salt covered the roads, the sidewalks were full of bundled-up pedestrians, and buses steamed at intersections.

We merged onto the freeway, and the city opened around us, its skyline jagged and beautiful beneath a soft curtain of snow. I couldn't help but be in awe of it. It was so different than Portland, different than Boston even.

I pulled out my phone and thumbed through a few notifications. A message from Jess—Text me when you're settled!—a calendar alert for the tour event tomorrow, and a news headline pinned to the top of my feed.

Chicago braces for early December snowstorm.

I tapped it open.

According to the forecast, a record-breaking cold front was expected to roll in over the weekend, dropping more than a foot of snow in parts of the city. Airports were already warning of delays. The article ended with shrugging reassurance that "Midwesterners know how to handle winter."

"Shit," I said quietly to myself as I let my head fall back against the headrest.

Darren glanced at me in the rearview mirror but didn't ask. I offered him a small smile, assuring him I was okay. He smiled back and kept driving.

The anxiety of an impending blizzard scenario threatened to swallow me whole, and manifesting no snow, no flight delays, and no canceled book tour was all I could do in that moment.

We pulled up to the entrance of the hotel. A valet opened the door for me, and I thanked Darren as I stepped out, the cold hitting me square in the chest.

I rolled my suitcase inside and was met with warm air and quiet music, the front desk glowing under soft lighting and a fake fireplace flickering behind glass.

Check-in was quick and easy. I took the elevator up to the 19th floor, room 1918.

As soon as I stepped in, I dropped my bags by the closet and stood there for a moment, still in my coat, hands in my pockets. The room was simple but comfortable, with gray bedding, a navy armchair, a small desk by the window, and a coffee maker I probably wouldn't use.

I pulled off my coat, boots, scarf, everything really, and let them fall in a soft heap by the door. Then I sat on the edge of the bed and let out a long breath I didn't know I'd been holding since I left home.

I set my phone down beside me, the screen still aglow with weather warnings and half-read messages, and crossed the room to the window.

It took both hands to pull open the heavy blackout curtains.

Outside, the city blinked back at me, alive and humming in the cold. The skyline stretched before me, wide and glittering. Everything felt sharp, outlined in white where the fallen snow had dusted the rooftops and fire escapes.

And there, piercing the night sky with its blinking red light, was the Hancock Building. I had recognized it from the guide pamphlets they had at the airport. Something about it made me pause: its height, its shape, the quiet pulse of the red beacon at the top like a heartbeat in the dark. All cities had that one thing that helped guide you home. It was a beacon.

Back in Massachusetts, it was the Prudential Center. And here, the Hancock Tower sat, tall and proud, keeping watch over its city.

I pressed my forehead lightly to the glass, suddenly homesick.

And a part of me liked to imagine he'd been looking at it too.

***

THEN — AGE 23

PORTLAND, MAINE

The diner was mostly empty that night, except for a few tired souls nursing mugs of coffee and a waitress with a fading wrist tattoo humming under her breath. We'd been coming here since we were kids. After school, after camp, after long nights we didn't want to end.

It was our place. This little corner booth with the squeaky vinyl and the personal table jukebox that still somehow worked, considering it was ancient. We always split a plate of fries and ordered two slices of pie to share. I couldn't count the number of times we'd sat here across from each other, laughing until our stomachs hurt or sitting in comfortable silence while the world spun outside the windows. No matter what else changed, this place had stayed the same.

We had both come home for the week to celebrate Christmas and we're still hungry after our own separate family festivities. Our booth was near the window, all fogged up from the outside chill. The fries were cold, the pies sat barely picked at, and my tea had gone lukewarm.

Miles hadn't said much in the last ten minutes, which wasn't unusual. He was like that sometimes, but tonight it felt different. He was fidgeting with the salt shaker and his fork like he was trying to distract himself from whatever he was thinking.

"Okay, Miles, you've been picking at that same piece of pie for like five minutes now. What's going on with you?" I finally asked, my irritation peeking out.

"I got an offer," he said finally, not looking at me.

I blinked. "What kind of offer?"

He shrugged, eyes still focused on the table. "An architectural firm in Chicago. They liked my portfolio, and I did a remote interview with them last week."

I sat back slowly. "Chicago?"

"Yeah."

The word hung there, unfamiliar and heavy, like it was a made-up place out of a storybook. I couldn't picture him there. Couldn't picture myself without him here. We weren't together; we never had been. But that didn't mean we weren't something. Something complicated, sure. But still something.

"How serious is it?" I asked.

He finally looked at me then. "Serious."

I tried to swallow the lump rising in my throat. "When would you go?"

"Sometime next year, after graduation, probably. If I take it."

"If," I repeated.

He nodded. Like we both didn't already know the answer.

The words barely registered at first. Not because I didn't hear them, but because I couldn't make any sense of them.

We had never been apart. Not for more than a few weeks. Not in any way that mattered. Even when I went to Italy the summer when we were sixteen, we still talked every day. I brought him back a keychain shaped like a Vespa, and he still had it hanging on the zipper of his old duffel bag.

We were constants. Background noise and lifelines. So the idea of him living in an entirely different city, living a life without him woven into mine, felt impossible. Like waking up and realizing you'd forgotten how to breathe.

I wanted to ask him not to go. I wanted to reach across the table and say, "You don't have to leave. Not yet. Not like this." But the words stayed locked behind my teeth, pressed down by the weight of everything we were and everything we weren't.

Because we had never been just friends, but we've never been anything else, either. And if I asked him to stay, and he missed out on this opportunity, what kind of person would that make me?

"I think you should do it," I said finally.

His eyebrows drew together, just slightly. "Yeah?"

"Yeah," I said again. "It's a big deal. I've seen how hard you've worked for this, Miles. You deserve this opportunity more than anyone."

He studied me like he didn't quite believe it. Or maybe he did. Maybe he was just waiting for me to say what I was really thinking.

But I didn't.

I couldn't.

So I picked up my mug instead, taking a sip of my now iced tea while my entire world began to crash down around me. "Chicago's a good city. I hear the architecture's incredible."

"Yeah," he said simply. "It is."

We paid the bill in silence. As he walked me to my car, I noticed that the snow had started to stick, clinging to the sidewalk in soft patches. My breath puffed into the air in short clouds. I didn't say anything when he leaned down to hug me. My hands clung to his coat without meaning to as I held on a little tighter than I normally would.

And when we pulled apart, he gave me a look I'd never forget. That soft, devastating look of someone who was saying goodbye without saying the word.

***

NOW

The city lights had blurred into a distant haze by the time I blinked back to the present.

The cold glass was fogged faintly from where my forehead had rested, and outside, the snow continued to fall. I stepped back from the window and glanced at the suitcase I hadn't touched yet, still propped upright against the wall. I didn't feel like unpacking, but I forced myself to do it anyway.

I unzipped the case and began folding clothes into the hotel's drawers. I unpacked jeans, sweaters, and the black boots I'd bought specifically for this trip. My thickest winter coat.

I laid out tomorrow's outfit on the back of the chair: dark jeans, a charcoal-gray turtleneck, and the comfortable black heels I only wore to book events. I planned on wearing minimal makeup and my hair down in some way. More to keep me warm than a style choice.

Everything felt routine. Automatic. Like my movement didn't quite belong to me in the moment.

When I finished, I stood in the middle of the room, arms crossed over my chest, staring at nothing. I hated the way being in a new place always made you feel like you were living a separate life from the one you'd grown accustomed to. I was expected to be someone more composed, more sure of herself. The version of me who was an author. A professional. Someone with answers.

But I didn't feel like her tonight.

I walked into the bathroom and washed my face, then brushed my teeth and let my hair fall loose from the tie I'd knotted it in earlier. My waves were frizzier than usual from the dry hotel air and the flight, but I didn't bother fixing them. I padded back into the room barefoot, the floor cold under my feet, and crawled into bed without turning off the lamp.

For a while, I just lay there.

Outside, the snow kept falling, turning the city into a dreamscape. From here, it looked like the world had been muted. Like everything below had gone quiet, just for me.

My phone buzzed just then. A text from Dylan.

> Dylan: Hey babe. Long day. Just got back. Hope you're settled in okay. Let me know how it goes tomorrow. Goodnight

I stared at the message for a moment, thumb hovering over the keyboard. Then I typed back:

Me: Landed safe. Hotel's nice. I'll call you tomorrow and fill you in. Love you.

I started to scroll aimlessly and check my notifications. I had received a text from Jess confirming the next day's schedule, and a few early reader comments had come in on my latest post. I liked a few without reading them.

Then I opened the Notes app.

There was a folder marked "Ideas" that I hadn't touched in months. Half-started blurbs. One-liners. Ideas and phrases I didn't want to forget. But nothing had stuck.

My next book was supposed to be some sprawling, whimsical slow burn with fake dating and a marriage pact. I had none of it drafted. My agent loved the premise. But I didn't feel it.

Not anymore. I hadn't in weeks.

I hesitated for a long moment, then tapped "new note." And without overthinking it, I typed three words.

That One Summer

That was all.

Not because I didn't know what came next, but because I did. And I wasn't sure if I was ready for it.

I locked the screen and set the phone facedown beside me.

The room was still. I so desperately wanted to succumb to sleep, but my brain was still humming. Wired with old memories, flickers of regret, and a skyline I didn't recognize.

I reached over and clicked off the lamp and watched as the room went dark.

And still, somewhere deep inside the quiet, I could hear his voice like it had never left.

Chapter 8

KEIRA

PRESENT DAY

CHICAGO, ILLINOIS

I woke to gray light spilling through the hotel curtains and the faint rattle of the vent kicking on.

For a second, I forgot where I was. The bed was too big. There were no sounds of coffee brewing in the kitchen, no Dylan rustling around in his usual half-awake shuffle.

Just a quiet hotel room, alone.

I stretched, rubbed my eyes, and sat up slowly, glancing at the clock on the nightstand.

7:04 a.m. Too early, but my nerves had been up since before the sun.

Today was officially the first stop on the tour.

I pulled my robe around me and padded across the cold floor to the little coffee machine by the dresser. Turns out it came in handy after all. It whirred to life with a sad sputter, spitting out a weak stream of light roast. I held the paper cup in both hands and stared out at the city while the windows began to thaw from the frost, revealing a sweeping view of downtown.

After a few minutes, I pulled myself away, stepped into the shower, and let the hot water shake off the last of the morning haze. Then I changed into the outfit I'd laid out the night before, trying to quiet the nerves already beginning to stir in my chest.

I clipped on a delicate pair of gold hoops, swiped on some mascara, and pulled my hair half up with a tortoiseshell pin. Professional but also somewhat casual. Just enough to feel like myself, or maybe a version of myself a little more polished than usual.

My phone buzzed on the counter. A message from Jess.

> Jess: Big day, YOU'VE GOT THIS BABE! Don't forget to breathe. Also, send pics!

I had a little over an hour to kill until my event. There was nothing left to do in the room except wait, and waiting was the last thing I wanted to do.

So I grabbed my key card and headed downstairs to the hotel lobby. The smell of fresh coffee hit me the second the elevator doors opened, and I followed it toward the small continental breakfast setup tucked beside the lounge.

There were only a handful of people seated. Mostly couples and business travelers who were halfway through their morning routines. I kept to myself, poured another cup of coffee, and fixed a small plate of fruit and toast.

I found a corner table by the window and ate slowly, letting the movement outside distract me. There were people rushing by in heavy coats, a delivery truck double-parked, and the quiet hum of a city that never really stopped. It grounded me, gave my thoughts somewhere else to go.

By the time I finished, the nerves had settled just enough to make me feel like I was ready for the day. I gathered my things, headed back upstairs, and before long, I was stepping out of the rideshare in front of the bookshop.

The building was small, brick-faced, and tucked neatly between a florist and a vintage thrift store. Above the door, a hand-painted sign read Oak & Sage Bookshop. But it was the window display that made me stop. It had been transformed into something I hadn't expected.

Something beautiful. Something just for me.

There, written in large gold letters across the glass and framed with hand-painted silver snowflakes, was my name.

KEIRA SULLIVAN: AUTHOR EVENT TODAY AND TOMORROW
Join us for a signing and Q&A at 1 p.m. on both days.

Below it were neatly arranged copies of both of my novels, propped up among string lights, paper flowers, and little handwritten cards with quotes from each book. One said, "Love is a risk. But some people are worth it."

It shouldn't have caught me off guard, but it did. Seeing my words like that, highlighted and celebrated, made something melt in my chest. It wasn't just that they belonged to me. It was that someone had read them, remembered them, and believed they mattered.

For a long moment, I didn't move. I just stood there on the sidewalk, staring through the glass with my heart lodged in my throat, trying to gather myself.

Then I took a breath, gripped the handle, and opened the front door.

Inside, it smelled like cedar and candles that had been burning a little too long. Warm. Familiar. Like if a library and a coffee shop had fallen in love. I absolutely loved it, and something in the atmosphere made me feel right at home. Wooden shelves lined the narrow walls, organized not just by genre but with staff picks and little handwritten notes tucked between spines.

There was a back table set up already with a chair, a stack of my books, and a pitcher of water with two glasses. A girl about my age with a pixie cut and cat-eyeglasses looked up from the register and smiled wide.

"You must be Keira," she said, stepping out from behind the counter. "I'm Ava. I've been dying to meet you!"

She ushered me toward the table, offering tea and snacks, and ran through the plan for the day with an efficiency that made me grateful I wasn't in charge.

A few early readers were already peeking in through the window. I felt the usual flutter of nerves creep up my spine, the perfect mix of imposter syndrome and performance anxiety that never really went away.

This was my second book tour. I'd done this before, so I understood the routine and the rhythm of it. But somehow, it still felt like the first time. The nerves always crept in, reminding me that I was still new at this. Still figuring it out. My career was just beginning, and with every event, every signing, it felt like I had something to prove.

***

By noon, the store had filled out. People sipped complimentary cider in little compostable cups and milled between the shelves. I sat behind the table, pen in hand, my stack of books slowly shrinking. I smiled. I chatted. I signed names and answered questions. Some readers wanted pictures. A few had tears in their eyes when they told me what the books had meant to them.

But it was one girl, maybe twenty-one or twenty-two, who stayed with me after.

She wore an oversized corduroy jacket and had a pin on her bag that read Books Save Lives. She waited until the others had trickled off, hovering near the back of the line like she wasn't sure if she belonged. When she reached me, she set down a copy of my second book and didn't speak right away.

"Hi," I said gently. "Want it personalized?"

She nodded, still quiet.

"What's your name?"

"Madison," she said, almost a whisper.

"Hi, Madison." I started to write, giving her my warmest smile.

"I just wanted to say…" she began, voice catching. "Your first book. I read it during a really hard time. Like, really bad. I'd just gotten out of the hospital. And it…I don't know. It made me feel like I wasn't completely alone."

I looked up.

She wasn't crying, but she was close.

I set the pen down and met her eyes. "Thank you so much for telling me that," I said.

I didn't pry into whatever she had experienced. I just smiled at her as best as I could.

She gave a small, trembling smile in response, "You're the reason I started writing again."

"Don't ever stop," I managed to say after I handed her the book.

She left quietly. I watched her disappear between shelves, then out the door.

The room kept moving, readers still mingling, Ava refilling cider, but something in me had gone still. Not in a bad way. I just felt full.

I'd needed that. I hadn't realized how much.

After the signing, Ava gave me a little wave from the back corner when it was time to start setting up for the panel. I stood, stretched my spine, and followed her past the shelves into a cozier side room lit crowded with mismatched chairs under pendant bulbs. The store had squeezed in about twenty people, all bundled in scarves and coats, cupping drinks and flipping through their dog-eared copies of my books.

Jess would've called this "intimate." She would've meant small. But I thought it was perfect.

I sat at the front while the audience was seated in chairs facing me in a semicircle. Some listeners filled the aisles. The conversation was casual but thoughtful. We talked about the pressure to always be working, about writing through burnout, and about the strange expectation that stories should be neat when real life never is.

I answered questions I'd heard a hundred times before, but tonight, they felt more personal. I shared how my first book came from relationship grief, how I still felt unsure of myself on most days, and how sometimes writing felt like trying to remember a dream you never actually had. There were a few laughs. A few knowing nods.

We were about twenty minutes into the panel when someone raised their hand from the second row. A woman around my age, wearing a chunky green sweater and holding a notebook in her lap.

She smiled nervously. "This might be kind of cliché, but…what made you want to be a writer? Like, what was the moment?"

There was a low murmur of agreement from the rest of the audience. People leaned forward a little. I shifted in my seat, buying time with a sip of water.

"That's a good question," I said, a little surprised by the swell of emotion it stirred in me. "I don't think I have just one moment. But I do remember the first time someone supported my writing enough to make me believe in myself."

I paused, searching for the right words. My fingers curled around the edge of my chair. It was an easy memory to remember. One I'd probably never forget.

***

THEN — AGE 13

CAMP RUSHWOOD, SEBAGO, MAINE

"Miles, come on. It'll be fun," I said, dragging him by the sleeve across the dirt path toward the little craft cabin where the writing group met every Wednesday morning.

He made a face. "I thought we were gonna go down to the lake."

"We still can after! It's only an hour. And there are snacks." I gave him the look. The one that always worked.

He groaned but didn't pull away. "Fine. But I swear, Keira, if they make me write a poem or something—"

"They won't," I said, though I wasn't totally sure. "It's just stories. You can write anything."

When we walked in, there were about ten kids already there, all sitting at folding tables with paper and pencils. Miss Brianna, one of the counselors, smiled and handed us each a worksheet.

"Today, we're writing about adventure," she said. "Real or imaginary."

I bounced a little in my seat, already thinking. Miles slumped into the chair next to me like he was being punished.

I looked at Miles. "Wanna write it together?"

"What if we don't agree on stuff?"

"That's the point. It'll keep things interesting."

He gave a dramatic sigh, but nodded. We ended up on the floor near the big bay window with a shared notebook between us, each of us taking turns writing a few lines.

At first, it was awkward. Miles didn't know what to say and tried to write about a two-story tall skate park in Tokyo, which I immediately vetoed, but then something clicked.

And it turned into a story.

Our characters were named Zoe and Theo, because those names sounded cooler than ours. They were best friends who decided that the second they graduated high school, they'd leave their small town and never come back. They had a list of countries and a jar full of change, and dreams way too big for the small town they lived in.

They would swim in hot springs in Iceland and take a cooking class in Paris and eat pistachio gelato in Italy. They'd ride a camel in Morocco and waddle with the penguins in Antarctica. They'd learn how to say "thank you" in twenty languages. They'd eat fries in Belgium, fall asleep on trains, and get matching tattoos in Barcelona that said "Not all who wander are lost," even though neither of us was sure what that actually meant. I just remembered reading it in a book once.

Their van was sea-foam green and covered in stickers from every place they'd been. Inside the glove compartment, they kept postcards they never sent and little napkins with silly doodles on them. Keepsakes of their time together, living their life on the road.

We didn't write the ending. We didn't want to. We just decided that they should keep going. I was so wrapped up in it that I didn't notice we were the only two still working long after the others had gone to the lake.

Miles leaned back, cracking his knuckles. "I can't believe we wrote all that."

"It's good," I said, flipping through the filled pages, amazed by how quickly it had come.

"You're good," he corrected. "You wrote all the cool parts."

I shook my head. "You wrote the part about the monkey stealing their map in India."

He smiled, and it reached his eyes. That didn't happen often. "Yeah, but you made it feel like it was real."

There was a long beat of quiet. I thought he'd start talking about something else, like how weird Miss Brianna's bright purple hair color was or how hot it had been outside.

But instead, he looked down at the paper again, then back up at me. "You should be a writer. Like...for real."

I blinked. "You think?"

"Yeah. I mean, who else could make two fake best friends feel like actual people in an hour?"

I didn't know what to say to that.

So I didn't say anything. Just smiled.

Later that summer, when we snuck out to sit on the dock at night and talk about the future, he told me we were gonna do that trip someday. That we were gonna be like Zoe and Theo. Forever Travelers. And even though we were only thirteen, and the world was still so big and blurry and full of maybes, I believed him.

***

NOW

The bookstore was quiet again, the audience still watching me with satisfied expressions. I blinked slowly, grounding myself.

"I think that was the first time I really felt it," I said aloud. "That stories could come out of me. That they could be something. And it felt good having that reassurance, even at such a young age."

A few people smiled. One woman in the back nodded like she understood exactly what I meant.

And somewhere inside me, I could still feel his voice at thirteen, so sure of me.

You should be a writer.

Eventually, the panel ended, and the crowd thinned. I found myself back at the main table, gathering the last of my things. The store had dimmed, the music lowered to a soft hum of jazz through the overhead speakers. I thanked Ava and told her I'd see her tomorrow for my last event in Chicago. Then I'd be off to the next stop on the tour

She handed me a small paper bag before I left. "Just something from the staff," she said, grinning. "A little Chicago thank-you from us here at the shop! See you tomorrow."

Inside was a chocolate bar, a single-use hand warmer, and a postcard with the skyline printed in watercolor. I felt my throat tighten unexpectedly.

"Thank you," I managed.

Outside, the snow was still falling in thick, heavy flakes and was starting to stick. I zipped my coat all the way up, pulled my scarf close, and tucked the paper bag under my arm as I stepped into the dark.

Back in the hotel, I peeled off the day in layers. Heels first. Then the jeans and sweater. After, I slipped into a worn sweatshirt and sweatpants, tied my hair into a loose bun, and made a cup of peppermint tea from the tray by the minibar.

The room was dim and quiet again. But this time, it didn't feel quite so heavy.

I curled up in the armchair by the window with the tea and my laptop balanced on the armrest. The skyline glittered just beyond the glass, and far in the distance, the Hancock Building continued its blinking, letting me know it was there for me.

My inbox was full of emails from Jess, tour logistics from Maya, and an enthusiastic subject line from my editor with three exclamation points, but I didn't open any of them.

Instead, I opened the note I'd started the night before.

I stared at it for a long time, but I didn't write anything new.

I didn't close it either.

I just left it there, waiting, as I let the night stretch around me.

I thought about Madison. I thought about the people who had come in out of the cold just to meet me. The bookstore window with my name spelled in gold.

And for the first time in a long while, I felt...good.

Like maybe, for today at least, I could breathe.

The thoughts I didn't want, the ones I'd been trying not to think for weeks, stayed in the background. Not gone, not forgotten. But less in the forefront of my mind.

I was grateful for that. Grateful for the distraction. For the noise of the day. For the readers who gave me something else to carry, just for a little while.

I turned off the light and slipped into bed.

Tomorrow would come fast, another busy day, then I'd be off to the next city.

But tonight, I let myself sleep.

Chapter 9

MILES

PRESENT DAY

CHICAGO, ILLINOIS

I couldn't sleep.

My mind kept circling the same thoughts, refusing to settle. I knew tomorrow was going to be a big day and I needed the rest, but all I could do was replay yesterday on a loop. I hadn't meant to take a different way home, but I drifted down a few side streets without thinking. I stopped cold when I saw her, and for a moment, it felt like the whole world stopped with me.

YESTERDAY

I woke up before my alarm, which was unusual for me.

There was something about mornings in the dead of winter, with its gray skies and promise of snow, the city not fully awake yet. I couldn't explain it. It's just one of those days where my chest didn't feel as heavy when I breathed in.

It was the kind of morning that made you think something good might actually happen, even if you didn't know what.

I stretched, ran a hand through my hair, and wandered into the kitchen in my socks. The tile was freezing, and the coffee maker made that horrible sputtering noise it always did when it was trying too hard, but even that didn't irritate me today.

I flicked on the TV, mostly for background noise while I waited for the coffee to finish brewing. The morning news was already in full swing, anchors talking over each other about some massive blizzard crawling its way across the Midwest.

"—expected to be the largest December snowstorm in over a decade, with Chicago right in its path."

Great. I was sure flights would be a mess. Streets worse.

I leaned against the counter and let the steam from my mug warm my face, watching the radar swirl red and blue across the screen. A little part of me almost liked the idea of being snowed in. It was a good excuse to hole up with bad takeout and avoid the world for a while. It would be nice not to have to go into the office. Even if it was for a day or two.

My phone buzzed on the counter.

Harper: Don't forget, Margo's at 11. If you're late, I'm ordering for you. And you know I will pick the worst thing on the menu.

I huffed a laugh into my cup. She wasn't wrong. Last time I flaked, she sent me a picture of cold oatmeal and a single slice of grapefruit.

I met Harper at a mutual friend's birthday party last year at some rooftop thing in the West Loop with overpriced cocktails and too many people pretending to have fun. She was easy to talk to, sharp in a way that kept me on my toes, and she didn't ask a lot of questions, which I appreciated.

We started texting, grabbed a drink once or twice, and eventually fell into something casual. She'd come over some nights, we'd sleep together, maybe order takeout or watch a movie.

It wasn't serious, but over time, it became a routine. Comfortable, in a way. But it never felt like more than a way to fill that lonely feeling. I think she hoped it would turn into something else. But I knew it wouldn't. I just couldn't imagine a future with her in it.

That probably made me an asshole, but I didn't have space for pretending.

I showered, got dressed, and pulled on my boots by the door while the weather app loaded. Still just gray skies for now, but the radar didn't look great. Snow was crawling closer, slower than expected but steady.

I grabbed my coat and stepped out into the cold with a to-go mug in one hand and my earbuds in the other.

The city on a Sunday was always my favorite. It was peaceful with the gentle buzz of residents wandering around and less rushed than normal, me being one of them. I liked it best like this. Just me, my footsteps, and the sound of tires hissing through slush before the brunch crowd swarmed the sidewalks, before everyone started being strictly business.

I got to Margo's a little after eleven. Harper was already inside, seated at one of the corner booths with her coat draped over the back and two mimosas already sweating on the table.

"You're late," she said when she saw me, smiling around the rim of her glass. "By only like—" She checked her phone dramatically, "—four minutes. I almost ordered you something terrible on principle."

I slid into the booth across from her. "Hey, at least I made it this time."

She pushed one of the glasses toward me and grinned. "True. You're lucky I'm merciful."

Harper always cleaned up to look her best, and today was no

different: a black cable-knit cardigan, gold hoops, perfect eyeliner. She was a beautiful woman; there was no denying that, even in the mornings when she woke up with a messy ponytail and mascara streaked from the night before.

I probably looked like I'd rolled out of bed and remembered how to function somewhere between brushing my teeth and pouring coffee. Which wasn't entirely wrong.

We made small talk while we looked at the menu. Weather. Work. A friend of hers who just got engaged. I nodded where I was supposed to, threw in the occasional joke to make her laugh.

It wasn't hard. It never was with her.

"You seem different today," Harper said, her eyes flicking up from her menu.

"Different how?"

"I don't know. Less broody than usual?" She smiled, but it tilted a little. "It's not a bad thing. Just...unusual."

I shrugged and sipped the mimosa. "Maybe I'm just enjoying the peace before the storm."

She rolled her eyes. "Is that a weather pun?"

"Might be."

I ordered the eggs Benedict. She got the avocado toast and made fun of herself for being a walking stereotype. We lingered over coffee after we ate, talking about the storm and whether she should stock up on canned food or just commit to wine and frozen pizza.

"You know," she said after a pause, "I think I like this version of you. You're pleasant to be around."

"Oh, thanks, and I thought you were just in it for the free meals," I said, rolling my eyes and throwing a smirk her way.

"Well, that too," she said, laughing quietly.

I may have laughed it off, but the words stuck with me longer than I expected. *This version of you.* I didn't ask what she meant, but I knew.

I'd been lighter the last day or two, less tense than usual, I guess. I hadn't noticed the shift myself until she pointed it out. Maybe it was taking that trip out of the city. Maybe it was the fact that things were going well at work. Or maybe it was something I wasn't aware of just yet.

Either way, she was right. I felt...better. Like something had loosened in my chest without me even realizing it. And that was rare for me. Rare enough that I didn't want to think too hard about why.

The waitress dropped the check, and Harper snagged it before I could reach for it.

I leaned back in the booth, watching her scribble a smiley face next to the total.

"You know," I said, "you make it difficult for me to be a perfect gentleman. It's my turn next time."

She laughed, then looked up at me with something softer in her eyes. "So...if the blizzard does hit like they're saying it will—" She paused, twirling the pen between her fingers, " —you thinking of hunkering down here in the city? Or are you heading out to your mom's?"

Shit. I knew where this was going.

"I'll probably stay," I said. "I've got to make sure I'm close to the office. And I wasn't planning on heading back to Portland this year. Maybe next Christmas."

I hadn't been home since I left. Every year, I'd tell myself I'd go back for the holidays. I'd book the flight, pack a bag, and sometimes even pick up one of those awful, overly sweet smelling candles for my mom. But every year, I'd find a reason not to. Work deadlines. Ticket prices. The weather. Some vague excuse about how the airports are always too chaotic around the holidays to leave.

I'd tell myself I'd be ready next time. That the distance is temporary. That life just gets busy.

But five years was a long time to stay gone.

And I think, deep down, some part of me knew I'd stayed away because going back would mean confronting the version of me that never really left.

The one still sitting next to her on that porch. The one who made the decision to walk away and not look back. She deserved more than someone who let fear make his choices for him. I should've been able to tell her how I felt, but the truth is, I was terrified of rejection. I was terrified of losing what we did have, of finding out I wasn't someone worth choosing. And that shame is the reason I can't bring myself to go back.

"Well, if it does snow you in, you could always…I don't know. Stay at my place. If you want."

Harper said it lightly, almost casual, but her eyes told me what she really wanted. And it was something I couldn't give her.

I stared down at the mug between my hands that had now gone cold.

"Yeah," I said, slow and careful. "Maybe. I'll think about it."

Her smile didn't falter, but she leaned back like she was bracing for something. "No pressure. Just figured it might be nicer than riding it out alone."

I nodded, and neither of us said much after that.

We both stepped back out into the cold and stood awkwardly outside the restaurant while the wind picked up around us. She hugged me goodbye, arms looping loosely around my waist, and I hugged her back with one arm, the other still in my coat pocket.

"Text me later?" she asked.

"Yeah," I said. "I will."

I watched her walk away down the block, her scarf blowing behind her like a ribbon.

And for a second, I thought about saying her name. Calling her back. Trying, really trying, but the words never left my mouth.

After that, I didn't feel like heading straight home.

Brunch had left me full but restless, like my body had too much energy and nowhere to put it. The air was colder now, the wind picking up in little bursts that stung my ears and made my coat feel too thin. I pulled my hood up, shoved my hands into my pockets, and walked.

I took a different route than usual. Down Oak, then across Belview. I couldn't say why I chose that route. Maybe it was the weather; the impending blizzard kept me from thinking straight.

The street was quiet, only a few people out, bundled up and moving quickly. Most of the shops were lit with that cozy amber glow and holiday lights. It made me almost feel the slightest twinge of Christmas spirit. I was halfway down the block when something in the window of a bookstore caught my eye.

Bright sticky notes. A handwritten sign on a table. A stack of books arranged neatly. And there, painted in large gold letters on the glass:

KEIRA SULLIVAN: AUTHOR EVENT TODAY AND TOMORROW JOIN US FOR A SIGNING AND Q&A AT 1 P.M. ON BOTH DAYS.

I stopped walking and felt my stomach drop.

Keira.

It couldn't be her. Couldn't possibly be *that* Keira.

I stared at the sign, at the name, and tried to make sense of it. My mind raced to logical explanations. Maybe it was someone else with the same name. Maybe it was a completely crazy coincidence. Sullivan was a common last name, right?

But my feet were already moving.

I stepped closer to the window, squinting past the glare of the overhead lights and the condensation creeping up the inside of the glass.

People were milling around inside, some setting up chairs, others chatting near the counter. There was a folding table near the back with stacks of books arranged in tidy towers, a silver thermos covered in stickers, and a small silver name placard.

And behind it, standing with her back slightly turned, laughing at something someone said, was her.

Keira. My Keira

Her hair was longer. She wore a soft turtleneck, dark jeans, and heels that made her look a little taller. She moved like she always had, unhurried, like she had all the time in the world.

She looked more beautiful than she ever had.

My breath caught.

Five years. I hadn't seen her in five years.

And now she was here. Alive, in the same space as me, separated only by a pane of frosted glass.

She didn't see me. And I didn't move.

I just stood there, heart pounding right out of my chest, watching her through the window.

For a second, the air felt too thin. My body was here, on this sidewalk, in this coat, in this city. But my mind was somewhere else entirely. Back at the lake. Back in her bedroom, listening to records. Back in the space where her name still meant something more than past tense.

I wasn't ready for this.

I checked the time. 12:36 p.m. I thought about walking away. Just turning around and pretending I hadn't seen any of it. But my legs stayed planted. Frozen.

She picked up a pen, uncapped it, and tested the ink on a sticky note, still completely unaware of me standing there. And somehow, that made it all harder.

I stepped back from the window, and the cold hit sharper than before, like I'd forgotten how bitter it was until I moved away from her.

Snow had started to fall, leaving damp traces on my shoulders and cheeks as I stood there, trying to catch my breath.

Across the street, the park was mostly empty. Just a few scattered benches, a crooked lamp post, and a fresh dusting of snow. I crossed over without thinking and dropped onto the nearest bench, the metal freezing even through my coat.

From here, I could see the bookstore. She was still behind the table, talking, laughing, flipping through one of her books like it wasn't strange to be here. Like no time had passed.

I stared at my hands, elbows resting on my knees. Everything felt like too much and not enough all at once. We hadn't spoken since the week I left. I didn't know where she went after, or what she'd been doing, or how she ended up here. I didn't even know she was publishing anything.

And then, suddenly, I wanted to know everything about her life in the last five years.

I wished she knew how proud I was of her. She'd made it happen for herself. She'd become a successful author. I always knew she would, but seeing it in real life was something else.

Part of me wanted to get up. Cross the street. Open the door and see what would happen.

But another part of me, the part that had taken control, knew I wasn't ready. And I wasn't completely sure if she would be either. So I sat there for a while and thought about it. Letting the cold sink in. Letting the sky grow darker around me as the storm loomed. Letting the thought of seeing her again slowly settle in my mind.

Eventually, I stood up.

I took one more glance at the window, then pulled my coat tighter and turned toward home.

Tomorrow, I was coming back.

Chapter 10

KEIRA

PRESENT DAY

CHICAGO, ILLINOIS

The bookshop felt cozier than the day before, with the snow falling heavier now. Mounds had started to build up on the sidewalk, and cars created brown slush that filtered through the street.

It was my last full day in Chicago. Tomorrow morning, I'd be on a plane to New York, and the whirlwind would start all over again. But right then, I was behind a table near the back of the shop, signing copies of my first book, *The Art of Falling in Love*.

We were already deep into the afternoon's scheduled signing. I had my hands wrapped around a hot chocolate and chatted with my readers as each one approached, learning all the different ways that my books had affected them positively.

I felt like I had made a difference in some small way, and I couldn't help but smile at the thought of that.

"Could you sign it to Liv?" the woman in front of me asked.

"She's my best friend. We read it together and basically screamed about it over FaceTime."

I smiled, uncapped my pen, and wrote a quick note on the title page. "Of course. That's one of the nicest things anyone's said all week."

The woman beamed, thanked me, and moved on. The line behind her was shorter now, with only a few people left. The staff was starting to shift gears, quietly setting up for the Q&A panel that would start in twenty minutes. I reached for my water bottle and let the tension ease out of my shoulders.

"Doing okay?" one of the bookstore staff asked as she passed by the table, holding a clipboard and a half-eaten granola bar.

"Yeah," I said. "I'm good, just a little tired. But it's been great. My social battery just isn't what it used to be."

She smiled. "Well, the turnout's been great. Chicago's clearly in love with you."

I smiled back, even though something in me flickered at the word love.

I'd just signed the last book and leaned back a little in the folding chair, flexing my hand, which was stiff from signing so many books. I glanced around the shop, admiring the comfort of it all. Wooden floors, string lights draped across the tops of the shelves, different themes with books to match, decorating the front panels of the aisles. It was the kind of place I would've loved even if I weren't here as an author.

There was something about it that reminded me of being seventeen again, wandering through small bookstores on the weekends, picking up hardcovers and special editions I couldn't afford and reading the first chapter, not having anywhere in particular to be. It made me miss my own little bookshop back home on the coast.

This was the part of the event where I usually relaxed. When the lines were gone, the table was cleared, and I could just exist for a minute before switching gears.

I started gathering the pens and sticky notes, tucking everything back into the pouch in my tote. Ava had left a chocolate on the edge of the table with a little "You survived" Post-it. I smiled at it without thinking.

Then I heard a voice behind me, a voice that couldn't possibly be here.

"Got time for one more?"

My hand stopped mid-reach, and suddenly, I was paralyzed.

I didn't know why right away, only that something in the sound hit me hard. My breath caught like it had been pulled out of me and held just out of reach.

I turned my head slowly.

He was standing just a few feet away, hands in the pockets of his coat, a cautious and awkward look in his eyes, like he wasn't sure if he should be here.

Miles.

When our eyes met, I saw those same blue eyes I'd known my whole life.

He looked the same, but slightly older. More mature even. His hair was perfectly tousled and a little shorter than he used to wear it, making his jaw look more defined. He wore dark jeans that hugged his legs and a thick black winter coat. He looked tired, with dark circles under his eyes. Or maybe that was just me projecting.

I didn't know what to say. I didn't know how to breathe.

For a second, all I could do was stare.

I blinked like it might clear the image, but it didn't.

"Hey," he said, unsure. "It's really you."

I nodded before I could speak, my mouth dry, my fingers still curled around the strap of my bag.

"Hi," I said finally. It was the only word I could manage to get out.

The world hadn't shifted. Nothing dramatic happened. The

bookstore was still here. People were still talking. The snow hadn't stopped. In fact, the wind started to pick up.

And inside this quiet little bookshop, inside of me, something cracked wide open.

"Hi," I said again, quieter this time. Because my brain still hadn't caught up with what was happening, and my mouth didn't trust itself to do anything else.

Miles didn't move closer, but he didn't back away either. He just stood there, watching me like he was trying to make sense of it too.

"I uh—wasn't sure if I should come in," he said after a beat. "I actually saw the sign yesterday, but I didn't want to interrupt when you had just started."

I nodded slowly. My heart was still somewhere in my throat, beating too hard for how still I was standing.

"I didn't know you were still in Chicago," I said, adjusting slightly. Well, of course not, cause how would I?

Miles gave a small nod. "Yeah. Still here." He looked down at the copies of my books, picking one up and turning it over in his hand. "I didn't know you were still writing."

"Yup. Still writing." I picked at the corner of a sticky note on the table. "Turns out I had a lot to say."

He gave a small, crooked smile. "That doesn't surprise me. You always did."

The silence stretched, and I didn't know what I expected from this moment.

Mostly, I felt off balance. Like I'd opened a door that had been nailed shut for years and was just now remembering how it used to feel to stand in that room.

Someone called my name from across the room. Ava, waving a clipboard gently in the air, reminded me that the Q&A panel was starting in a few minutes.

I looked back at Miles, pointing to the back room. "I should—"

"Yeah, of course." He took a step back, giving me space. "I didn't mean to derail anything."

"You didn't." I turned slowly, but I didn't walk away just yet. "Did you want to stay?"

"Sure, if that's okay," he said

I nodded, and a small smile started to break on my face. "Yeah. It's okay."

He found a seat at the back of the room and sat casually, like he hadn't just shaken something loose in me I'd spent five years trying, and failing, to ignore.

I sat at the front of the panel, smiled when I was introduced, and answered the first question automatically.

But the whole time, I could feel his eyes on me.

And all I could think was: *He's here. He's really here.*

***

The panel was starting to wind down. People were still engaged, but the energy in the room had settled into less excitement and more reflection. It all felt more relaxed after the big laughs and easy questions had passed.

The bookshop owner announced, "We have time for one or two more," she said, scanning the hands that had gone up.

She pointed to someone near the back. A girl in a denim jacket with a soft voice and a notebook in her lap.

"What would you tell your younger self if you could?" she asked.

I sat with it for a moment, unsure of how honest I wanted to be. I could hear the murmur of traffic outside. I could still feel Miles' eyes on me, waiting.

I looked down at my hands, then lifted my eyes back to the group.

"I think I'd tell her that it's okay to not have it all figured out," I said. "That life has a way of surprising you when you least expect it."

I paused, and for a second, the room felt far away. I suddenly looked up and met Miles' eyes.

I cleared my throat gently. "I think I'd tell her to take more chances. Because not every door stays open forever."

***

THEN — AGE 24

ONE WEEK AFTER THE MOVE

It had been seven days.

Seven days since I hugged him goodbye, pretending I wasn't memorizing the way his sweatshirt smelled or how it felt when he held me. Seven days since I watched him disappear through airport security with a carry-on slung over one shoulder and his jacket tied messily around his waist, like it was no big deal. Like he wasn't about to leave for good.

We talked a couple of times after he moved. Nothing heavy. Just a few casual messages here and there. I asked how the apartment was. He said the city was loud. I sent back something about the weather.

Then it slowed. Days passed between replies. Eventually, he sent one last text that said he hoped everything was good on my end. I stared at it for a while before typing "Thanks. It's as good as it can be," and hitting send.

And that was it. That was the last time we talked.

It crept in slowly at first, disguised as space.

I told myself it was normal. That he was settling in, adjusting, figuring things out. I didn't want to be the clingy friend who made it about me when he'd just made a huge life change.

So I waited. I gave it a day. Then another. Then three more. And by the time I realized how badly I wanted to hear his voice, it felt too late to ask for it.

I was lying on my bed one night, staring at the ceiling, my phone resting on my stomach like it weighed ten pounds.

The room felt too quiet. My body felt too still. Outside, I could hear cars passing and the occasional burst of laughter from someone on the sidewalk. The rest of the world was moving forward like nothing had happened.

But I was stuck here, in the space he used to fill. In our apartment, which now felt lonelier than ever.

I missed him so much it made my heart physically hurt. Like missing him had woven itself into my day.

I'd go to tell him something, only to remember I couldn't. I'd pass a coffee shop and think of that time he spilled an entire latte in his lap and still insisted he'd "handled it gracefully."

I'd laugh at something, then feel the quiet hit a little harder when no one laughed with me.

I missed his dumb jokes and his terrible handwriting. I missed how he always offered me the last bite even though I knew he wanted it. I missed the way he saw through me without ever making me feel too exposed.

But mostly I missed him in that deeper, intimate way I hadn't been brave enough to say out loud while he was still here.

I knew I loved him.

I had for a long time, even if I'd tried to tell myself it was just a phase. Just a comfort. Just something that would eventually fade.

But it hadn't faded.

If anything, it was louder now. The distance had only made the truth harder to hide from.

We had always been something, we both knew that, but we never said it. Never spoke about it.

I reached for my phone again and opened his name in my messages. Our final text still sat near the top, tormenting me. I must have looked at that message a hundred times that week, waiting for it to transform into something else.

I started typing.

Hey. I miss you.

Backspaced.

Tried the place on 8th again today. Still not as good without you.

Backspaced again.

I sat there staring at the blinking cursor, heart thudding in my chest like something trying to escape. I wanted to call him. I wanted to hear his voice and ask how he was doing and tell him I wasn't okay, and I didn't think I would be until I knew how he felt.

But I couldn't do it.

I was scared of what he wouldn't say. Of what silence might mean. Of hearing kindness in his voice but nothing more. I was scared I'd ask for something I wasn't sure that he could give me.

I mean, if we were meant to be together, how come we never really tried after twelve years of being...whatever we were?

I never knew how to explain it other than that the timing never felt right. There was always something in the way, whether it be school, relationships, or the fear of messing up our friendship. I kept telling myself we'd figure it out when life finally settled down. But the truth was, life never really settled. And maybe we were just scared. Scared that something so big, so real, would unravel if we messed with it.

So we stayed what we were. Always caught in the in between.

I kept my phone close the rest of the night, like maybe he'd sense it somehow. Like the universe would nudge him to text me first. Just something small. Anything. A, "How are you?" even if it was out of obligation. I would've taken it.

But it never lit up.

The hours passed slowly. I didn't move much. Just lay there on top of the covers with the lights off and the ceiling fan circulating, all the while my mind was racing. I thought about all the things I should've said before he left. How I'd let the moment slip past me because I didn't want to ruin anything. I'd convinced myself there'd be time later.

That we'd find our way back, eventually.

But I was starting to realize that love didn't always wait for you to figure it out.

Sometimes, it drifted. Even if it didn't want to.

And sometimes, you let it go on that path for a while. Until there was nothing left.

I didn't sleep that night. I just watched the sky go from dark to gray and wondered if he was doing the same thing in some unfamiliar apartment a thousand miles away.

When the sun finally came up, I told myself I'd wait one more week. If I didn't hear from him by then, I'd let it go. I'd stop checking my phone. I'd stop hoping.

He never reached out.

Chapter 11

MILES

PRESENT DAY

CHICAGO, ILLINOIS

Sitting in the back of the room felt like the safest place to fall apart.

No one was paying attention to me, but why would they? The lights were warm and low, the chairs were arranged in a gentle semicircle, and all eyes were on her.

I hadn't expected to feel like this. I didn't even know what this was, just that something inside of me had softened the second I heard her voice again, and now I was sitting here trying to piece myself together without making it obvious.

She was glowing.

Not in a dramatic, cinematic way, but in a real way. An everyday way, if that made sense.

She was so confident. Her eyes were clear, her posture relaxed, her laugh softer but still full of life. She spoke with ease, smiled between answers, and made people feel seen without even trying.

I hadn't seen her in five years, and somehow she was both exactly the same and completely different, and I didn't know what to do with the fact that my body still recognized her like no time had passed at all.

I listened to her talk to the audience, answering their questions with a kind of openness that made it look easy, like being vulnerable in front of a room full of strangers was just another part of the job.

She was so sure of herself. So present. I don't think I ever realized how much strength she carried in her voice until I heard it again after so long.

I was proud of her in a "God, just look at you, I always knew you could do this," type of way. This was me, sitting here in a corner of a bookshop, realizing I'd spent the last five years trying not to think about the one person who never really left my head.

So there I sat, quiet, still, hands resting in my lap, watching her answer another question with that honesty she always had, and I just let myself feel it. All of it.

And for the first time in years, I didn't try to turn away from it.

The panel wrapped up with polite applause and a few last-minute questions shouted as people stood to leave. Keira gave a small wave and a thank you, still smiling, still gracious, even though she looked tired now, like the adrenaline was wearing off and the hours were starting to catch up to her.

She stood slowly, collected her things, and chatted with one of the bookshop workers for a moment. Her posture shifted, becoming more casual now, more human.

The room buzzed with people gathering coats, stuffing signed books into tote bags, and filing out through the front doors with the kind of aimless conversation that always follows a good event.

I stayed in my seat and waited for the right time to approach her.

It was almost four, but the sky outside was already dimming. That winter kind of dark that creeps in before it's welcome.

The wind had picked up while we were inside, and the snow was falling hard. It collected at the windows and stuck to the shoulders of the people walking by, making everything look colder than it probably was.

Eventually, the room emptied down to us and the store manager.

She glanced over once and caught me still sitting here. I stood slowly, shoving my hands into my pockets to keep them from fidgeting.

"Hey," I said, walking over as the room finally emptied. "You were great."

She smiled, a little breathless. "Yeah?"

"Yeah," I said. "Really."

I hesitated, standing a little awkwardly to the side of her table, watching her zip up her tote and cap her pen. I wanted more time with her. She was here, right in front of me, and I couldn't walk away from her again. Not now.

So I gathered up my courage as best I could. "You, uh, want to grab a drink or something? Catch up a little?"

I wasn't sure if she'd say yes. But I knew if I walked out now, I'd regret it.

Keira looked up at me, thoughtful for a second, then tilted her head the way she always used to when she was considering something she already knew the answer to.

"Actually, I'm starving," she said. "And honestly? I could really go for a greasy burger and a chocolate shake right about now. Know anywhere around here that's good?"

A real smile tugged at the corners of my mouth before I could stop it.

"Still the same," I said, shaking my head.

"Still always hungry," she replied.

We both laughed, clearly surprised at the ease of conversation.

"I know just the place," I said.

Keira raised an eyebrow. "Is it actually good, or are you about to make me eat somewhere with peeling linoleum and three Yelp reviews? Like that place you found in Cambridge that one time—"

"Hey," I laughed, cutting her off. "That place was a gem. They just happened to have a roach problem. Not their fault, Cambridge can be dirty as hell."

That made her laugh again. It was this short, real sound that hit me square in the chest.

We stepped outside together, the bell over the bookstore door jangling as it shut behind us. The wind hit harder than I expected, a sharp slap of cold that got under my collar and bit at my ears. The snow was falling in thick, diagonal flakes that stung when they caught your face.

I pulled my hood up and glanced over at her. She was already wrapped tight in her coat, her scarf pulled halfway up her face, but her eyes were bright in that way they always got when the weather turned dramatic. Like she was more awake in the chaos.

The diner was only six blocks away, but the wind made every step slower.

Cars passed with tires driving through the slush, and the streetlights flickered on ahead of schedule, probably due to the storm.

"Is this normal for Chicago?" she asked, projecting her voice over the wind.

"I wish I could say no." I laughed. "But I will say that we haven't had a real storm like what's expected in a while."

I kept thinking about the blizzard. The news had been warning everyone the last few days, and the way the sky looked now made me believe them.

This wasn't the kind of snowfall that quietly faded by morning. This was the kind that trapped people. That canceled plans, grounded flights, and forced you to stay where you were, whether you wanted to or not.

I tried not to think too hard about that.

We didn't talk much on the walk. Just the occasional comment about how ridiculous the weather was, how dumb it was that we were out in it, and how good this burger better be after suffering through all of this. But it wasn't uncomfortable. The silence felt familiar. Like we hadn't gone five years without sharing it.

***

By the time we stepped into the diner, the windows had completely fogged over. The place was quiet and mostly empty except for a couple in a booth near the back and a kid behind the counter pretending to clean something while scrolling his phone.

It smelled like old coffee and French fry grease, which, if you asked me, was a fantastic, nostalgic smell. I hadn't been here in a long time, but it looked exactly how I remembered: red vinyl booths, wobbly tables, and a jukebox in the corner that hadn't worked since before I moved here.

"This is exactly the kind of place I was picturing," Keira said, unwinding her scarf. "Reminds me of our spot back home."

"You're welcome," I said, sliding into a booth by the window. "High-end dining experience, just for you."

She sat across from me, pulling her gloves off finger by finger and setting them on the table. Her cheeks were still red from the cold, and her hair was a little damp where the snow had started to melt.

"So," she said, flipping open the menu. "What's good here?"

I leaned back, lacing my hands around my head. "Depends on your definition of 'good.' But I've survived everything on the menu, if that helps. The waffles aren't too bad."

She smirked, eyes still scanning the page. "Waffles, huh? Bold choice."

I raised an eyebrow. "Bold? They're superior, and you know it. Crispy edges, golden squares, built-in syrup compartments. What more could you want?"

She looked up at me like I'd just said something deeply offensive. "Miles, we've had this argument before and determined you were completely wrong. Pancakes are the gold standard. They don't need compartments; they absorb the syrup. Efficiency."

"They sponge it," I said, wrinkling my nose. "It's like eating syrup-soaked cake. With waffles, there's balance."

"Balance," she repeated, deadpan. "You know you sound like a snob, right?"

"Waffle snob," I agreed, unapologetic. "I stand by it."

She laughed under her breath and set the menu down. "You always did have terrible taste."

"And yet here you are. At a diner I chose. With me," I said, grinning as I flagged down the waitress.

We skipped the heavily debated breakfast foods and went with our usual go-to—two burgers, two shakes, and a side of fries to share. The kind of meal we would've gotten without thinking back then.

When the waitress walked away, I rested my forearms on the table and looked at her.

"So. You actually did it," I said.

Keira blinked. "Did what?"

"Got published. Became an author." I nodded slowly. "I don't know what I expected today when I watched your panel, but...you were just...solid. Confident. It was cool to see."

Her expression softened. "Thank you. I was really nervous."

"You didn't look it."

"That's good to know. I was mostly running on caffeine and adrenaline," she said.

I smiled, but it faded gently. "I'm proud of you. I knew you always would be successful, but to see it in person for the first time—"

My words got lost then. She always had a habit of doing that to me.

She looked down for a second, then back up at me.

"Thanks," she said quietly. "That means more than you probably know."

The shakes came first. Two tall glasses with metal cups on the side, slightly sweating from the heat of the room.

Keira took one sip and sighed, like she'd just let go of all the stress that had been weighing on her shoulders.

"God, that's good," she said. "I haven't had one of these in forever."

"You used to make me drive across town for them," I said.

She leaned forward. "That was for a very specific seasonal mint shake," she said, raising a finger. "And it was important."

I shook my head, smiling. "It wasn't even good. I could literally taste the food coloring."

"It was festive. That was the whole point. Taste didn't matter."

We laughed, and just like that, the tension eased a little more. Something about sitting across from her again in this little city diner, talking about nothing, drinking something way too sweet. It made time stand still.

"So," she said, after a moment, resting her chin on one hand, "what's your life like now? I mean, outside of stalking authors at bookstore events."

I snorted. "Onetime offense."

She raised an eyebrow, waiting.

I shrugged. "It's...fine. I work for a firm here in the city. Mid-sized. We do a lot of commercial projects, but a few public spaces too. Parks, libraries, schools. I moved into a decent apartment about a year ago. Same neighborhood. Close enough to a train, far enough from tourists."

"Sounds very grown-up of you."

I nodded. "You could say that."

She smiled, but there was something quiet behind it. "You seem good."

"I'm trying." I took a sip of my shake to avoid responding too fast. "What about you?" I asked. "How's tour life treating you?"

She leaned back a little, letting her shoulders relax into the booth. "Chaotic. Exhausting. A little lonely, honestly. But also...kind of amazing. Some days I still can't believe it's real. Other days, I'm just trying to remember what city I'm in. This is only my second tour, and I think I'm finally starting to get the hang of it."

"And you leave tomorrow?"

"Well, I'm supposed to." She glanced toward the window where snow had started to build against the glass. "Though, if this keeps up, I might be stuck here a while."

I followed her gaze. The streets were starting to blur. Tire tracks vanished within seconds.

The sky looked bruised and heavy.

"Could be worse," I said.

She looked at me again, searching my face for something. I wasn't sure what.

"Yeah," she said softly. "It could."

Keira wiped her hands on a napkin and reached for her shake again, taking a long sip. Her eyes flicked toward the window and back. The diner had grown even quieter, just the low hum of fluorescent lights and the rattle of a dish bin in the back filling the empty space.

And then, without warning, she asked, "Are you seeing anyone?"

I looked at her for a moment, trying to gauge what kind of answer she wanted. Then I decided not to overthink it.

"No," I said. "Not really. There was someone...off and on. But it never stuck. I think we both knew it wasn't going anywhere. Other than that, nothing serious."

She nodded, slowly. Like she wasn't surprised.

I asked her the same question. "What about you?"

There was a pause.

Then she said, "I'm engaged."

I blinked. I wasn't expecting that, and neither was my heart, because I suddenly felt it stop.

Her tone was steady, but there was no smile to it. Just a fact laid gently on the table between us.

I nodded, slow. "Yeah?"

"Yeah," she said again, and then, "His name's Dylan."

She looked down at her hands, like they might explain something she couldn't put into words.

"That's really great, Keira," I lied, "How long have you two been engaged?" I asked carefully.

"About a year," she said. "We've been together for three."

I waited, but she didn't add anything else. No stories, no fond details. Nothing about how they met or what he was like. Just silence.

I looked down at her hand and found no engagement ring. She didn't have one on, and I couldn't help but wonder why.

In the silence that followed, I felt it.

Whatever this was, whatever they were, wasn't simple. She didn't say she was happy. She didn't say she was excited. And she didn't meet my eyes.

"You love him?" The words came out before I could decide whether to say them.

She looked up at me, and for a split second, I saw something flicker across her face.

"Of course I do," she said. "It's just...Sometimes I think I'm just trying really hard to make it work because it's supposed to. Because he's what's good for me. And he really is. He's a wonderful guy."

That sat between us, heavier than anything we'd said so far. I didn't push her on it, I just nodded like I understood. And I couldn't help but wonder if she was trying to convince me, or her.

To be honest, I didn't know what I expected from seeing her again. But sitting across from her now, watching her stir her shake, lost in thought, I realized something I hadn't wanted to admit until this exact moment.

I hadn't moved on.

And I hadn't gone into that bookstore for closure.

I went in because I still wanted to know her.

Because five years later, with a fiancé and a life I was no longer a part of, I was still looking at her like maybe—just maybe—it wasn't too late.

Chapter 12

KEIRA

PRESENT DAY

CHICAGO, ILLINOIS

It felt strange saying Dylan's name out loud to Miles.

I'd said it a hundred times over the past few years to customers at the shop, to my neighbors in Rockport, to strangers making small talk at book events, but this was different.

Miles didn't know anything about my life now. He didn't know about my little apartment above the bookshop I owned. He didn't know about my sweet pup, Lola, who was waiting for me back at home. He didn't know Dylan.

And somehow, saying I was engaged to the person who once knew me better than anyone felt like saying it for the first time, and in that, I was hearing everything I didn't want to admit right there in the echo of it.

I kept my voice even, but I could feel how hollow it sounded. I didn't look at him when I said it. I wasn't sure I could. Maybe because I knew the second I did, he'd see right through it.

I told him the basics. That it had been a little over a year. That things are good. That it made sense.

What I didn't say is that I've been second-guessing everything since the day we set a date. That some nights I stare at the ceiling in my apartment, listening to the bookstore creak below me, and wonder what it would feel like to want something with certainty again.

Dylan was good. Stable. The kind of man who never forgot to text me when he was running late. We got along and almost never argued. But lately, I'd felt like I was living someone else's version of happiness. Like I'd wandered into a life that looked like a postcard but didn't sound like me when I spoke to the outside about it.

I didn't tell Miles any of that.

But I think he knew.

He looked at me in a way when I said Dylan's name that was questioning, like he could still read me without trying.

And maybe that's what I'd missed the most.

***

By the time we left the diner, the world outside looked completely different.

The sidewalks had disappeared under a thick layer of snow, and the wind had picked up enough that I had to pull my scarf tighter just to keep it from slapping against my face.

Streetlights glowed dimly through the haze, casting everything in this soft, muted blur, like the city had been pulled underwater.

Miles walked beside me quietly, his shoulder close enough to feel even without touching. The cold bit through my coat, and I shoved my gloved hands deeper into my pockets, trying not to shiver.

I pulled out my phone to check the time and saw the flood of notifications all at once. I opened the dropdown and saw texts, emails, and weather alerts. I stopped walking.

"What is it?" he asked.

I scrolled through quickly. "My flight tomorrow. They canceled it. And there's an update from the airline about all flights being delayed until further notice."

"Shit, that bad?" he asked.

"Apparently." I clicked the email from my agent.

It was brief: *Call me when you can. NYC event postponed. Stay put until we figure things out.*

I sighed and tucked my phone away. "Well…looks like I'm not going anywhere."

Miles must've sensed the tension creeping into my shoulders and noticed the way I kept checking the time or picking at the sleeve of my jacket. He didn't say anything right away, just watched me for a moment, like he was weighing something.

Then, gently, he asked, "Would it be okay if I walked you back to your hotel?" I looked at him, surprised by how much I wanted to say yes.

"You sure?" I asked. "It's a little out of the way."

He shrugged. "I don't mind. Gives me a few more minutes with you."

I smiled, a little shy. "Yeah. I'd like that."

By the time we reached the hotel, the lobby was a mess. Power flickering, people crowding the front desk, voices overlapping. The building was running on backup, and half the elevators weren't working.

A tired-looking concierge told me my floor was without heat due to a blown transformer. Something about pressure shifts from the storm and a cracked outer window. It was safe, but it wasn't going to be comfortable to stay there that night, not unless I wanted to freeze.

I stepped away from the desk, trying to take a breath, but it caught in my throat.

This wasn't just inconvenient. It was literally—pun totally intended—snowballing out of control.

"Hey," Miles said quietly, stepping beside me. "You okay?"

"I don't know," I said, trying to laugh, but it came out brittle. "Apparently, my room's become a walk-in freezer, I don't have anywhere else to go, my flight's canceled, and everything going on in this building right now is making it hard to breathe."

His mouth pulled into a crooked half smile. "You always get weirdly specific when you're overwhelmed."

I shot him a look, but he was right. The stress wasn't helping anything.

"This is a disaster," I said softly.

"It's a storm," he replied. "And you've been through worse."

I swallowed hard.

"You're not alone, Keira. Not right now. Everything's going to be fine."

And something about being here now, in the middle of this mess, with him next to me again made everything slow down, just a little.

I took a deep breath. "Thanks," I said softly. "You always knew how to pull me out of my own head."

He looked at me then. "That's because I spent half my life living there."

Before I could even process what to say to that, my phone buzzed in my coat pocket.

Dylan.

I answered quietly. "Hey."

"You okay?" His voice was calm. "I just saw the news. Chicago's getting slammed. Are you still at your hotel?"

"Yeah," I said. "Kind of. I mean, I'm here, but there's a power issue, and my room's not usable. It's chaos."

"You're not going to try to get out of the city, right? Roads are already closing."

"No. I don't think I could even if I wanted to."

He let out a breath, "Alright. Just be careful, okay? Find somewhere safe to stay, and please, let me know as soon as you're settled."

"I will."

"I'll check in tomorrow. Stay warm. I love you."

"Okay. I love you too."

Click

I stared at my phone for a second longer than I meant to. Then slipped it back into my pocket and turned toward Miles.

He must've heard enough to read my face. His voice was gentle when he spoke.

"You can stay at my place."

I blinked at him.

"Just for the night," he added quickly. "Or longer, if this thing drags on. I've got heat, power, and a comfortable couch. You can stay in my guestroom. It even has its own bathroom."

I hesitated

Not because I didn't want to. But because I did, and I didn't know what that meant.

"You shouldn't have to figure this out alone," he added.

He was right. Realistically, what other options did I have?

"Okay," I said softly. "Thanks."

"No problem. Now let's get out of here before we get snowed in. My place isn't far."

***

THEN – AGE 16

PORTLAND HIGH SCHOOL WINTER RECITAL

I was going to pass out. I just knew it.

My heart wouldn't slow down. My hands were clammy and locked around the crumpled copy of my monologue, the words smudged where my thumb had rubbed the ink raw. I could hear the muffled sound of applause through the curtain as someone finished their piece. That meant I was next.

Oh God. I was next.

I hadn't wanted to do this. It wasn't my idea. The entire sophomore class had to perform something for the winter recital, and I'd gotten stuck with a monologue from some play I'd never even heard of. My English teacher called it "raw" and "powerful." I just thought it sounded like someone complaining about their life.

I couldn't do it. Not in front of all those people. Not with the lights and the silence and everyone watching like they expected something epic from me.

I slipped out of the wings when no one was looking, down the narrow backstage hall that smelled like paint and dust. My boots echoed against the floor until I dropped into a crouch, hiding behind a stack of unused risers, the monologue still clutched in my hand.

I curled my knees to my chest, trying to slow my breathing. But it wasn't working. My throat felt tight. My eyes were stinging.

You're fine, I told myself. *You practiced. You're overreacting.* But the more I said it, the worse it got.

Then a shadow fell across the wall.

I froze.

"Keira?"

I looked up and took a sigh of relief. It was Miles.

He didn't look surprised to see me crouching on the floor behind the risers. He just exhaled like he'd expected this.

Thankfully, he didn't laugh. He would never tease me like some guys might have.

He sat down next to me, arms resting across his knees. "You okay?" he asked.

I tried to answer, but my voice cracked. "I can't do it, Miles."

"Okay," he said simply, like that was a perfectly acceptable answer.

"You're not gonna tell me to suck it up?"

"Nope." He looked over at me. "But I can sit with you for a while until you make a decision on what you want to do."

I didn't say anything. I just nodded.

He reached into his hoodie pocket and pulled out his old wired earbuds; the left one was held together with electrical tape. He scrolled something on his iPod, then held one out to me.

"Here," he said.

I took it and tucked it into my ear.

"Here's to the Night" by Eve 6 started playing. It was one of our camp songs.

The music was slow and steady and made me think of all the fun summers we had. I was able to get lost in that moment. The sound curled around my panic like it was coaxing me back to earth.

I closed my eyes and let my head fall against his shoulder.

He didn't move.

We stayed there like that until someone else's monologue started. Until I could breathe again. Until the moment passed and I felt like me again.

***

NOW

By the time we reached his building, my scarf was damp, and my hair was clinging to the sides of my face. I decided to leave all my things there since I didn't relish climbing nineteen flights of stairs.

Miles held the door open, and I stepped into the lobby, grateful for the sudden rush of warm air that wrapped around me like a heated blanket. My skin prickled at the contrast.

A security guard sat behind a front desk, flipping through paperwork and nodding at Miles as we passed.

The space was quiet and clean, with tall ceilings, warm lighting, and modern fixtures. The faint sound of jazz could be heard playing over a speaker tucked somewhere out of sight. It was tasteful and sophisticated.

It all threw me for a second, since I honestly didn't know what to expect. Something older, maybe, a walk-up with creaky stairs and peeling paint. But this was definitely not that.

I adjusted the strap on my shoulder bag and took it all in as we crossed the space.

We took the elevator to the fourth floor. The hallway smelled faintly of laundry detergent and fabric softener, and when he unlocked the door and let me inside, my last bit of tension dropped away completely.

And—okay—I'll admit it. I was surprised.

The entryway was clean. Not just not messy...but actually clean. The shoes by the door were lined up neatly, and a coat rack hung just above a narrow bench with a folded umbrella beneath it.

As I stepped in farther, I took in the rest of the space: an open kitchen, spotless counters, a small living room with shelves that weren't crammed with junk. They were organized with art books, a few framed sketches, and even a plant that looked alive and thriving. A giant dark blue area rug stretched out invitingly and looked as if it were vacuumed daily.

I turned to him slowly with raised eyebrows. "Okay...who are you and what did you do with Miles Bennett?"

He let out a short laugh and kicked off his boots. "Wow. That didn't take long."

"I mean, I'm just impressed Miles! This is so...different." I gestured around the space. "No laundry mountain on the couch, no old pizza boxes, no thick smell of weed clinging to the furniture."

"I'll have you know I've grown," he said, tossing his coat onto the hook by the door. "I pay taxes and everything."

"God, you used to live like a gremlin. I distinctly remember a science project growing mold in a takeout container under your bed."

He sat himself on the couch and lifted his feet up. "That *was* an experiment."

I shot him a look. "Uh, no. It turned into an experiment because you forgot to throw it away."

He laughed, and I laughed too, and for a second, it felt easy. Like this was a night from years ago, and we were just picking up where we left off.

"Well," he said, "somewhere along the way I realized I actually appreciate a decent vacuum. That, and I learned pretty fast that women don't exactly line up to hang out in a disaster zone. So...I figured it was time to grow up a little."

"That make's sense," I said. I wandered through the rest of the apartment, admiring the space but slowly realizing just how much time had passed.

It still felt like him. Warm, thoughtful, and a little chaotic, but it also carried pieces of a life I hadn't been part of.

On the side tables were framed photos from nights out with friends I didn't recognize, snapshots of memories I hadn't shared. A postcard from Rome was pinned to a corkboard by the kitchen.

This wasn't just Miles's apartment. It was his life now. One that had gone on without me.

I started walking over to the couch when I saw it...something familiar. It was the honey pot lamp from our apartment.

I reached out and touched the corner of the lampshade, just to be sure it was real.

"I can't believe you kept this," I said quietly.

Miles' cheeks started to tinge red. "Yeah, it grew on me."

"Does it even still work?"

He shrugged, but there was a softness in his expression. "When it wants to. It's always kind of made every place feel more like home."

I nodded, letting that sit with me for a second.

"You were right, by the way. It does have character."

I grinned, just a little. "Took you long enough to admit it."

He laughed under his breath and nodded toward the hallway. "Guest room's that way. You want something dry to change into? I've got some sweats that will be comfortable enough for you."

"That'd be great," I said, smiling.

The guest room was small, but cozy. It had a full-size bed with a white-and-cream quilt tucked neatly at the corners, a nightstand with a little reading lamp, and a dresser that looked like it had belonged to someone's grandfather before being given new life with a coat of white paint. A window overlooked the snowy street below, the glass fogging slightly from the warmth of the room.

There was a bathroom attached. It was bright with warm yellow lighting and stocked. I peeked inside and found a folded towel on the rack, fresh soap, and even a little plant on the windowsill.

I turned when I heard a soft knock.

Miles pushed the door open with his elbow, arms full of folded clothes. He brought sweatpants, a hoodie, thick socks, and a long-sleeved t-shirt. He handed them over without making a big deal about it.

"Here," he said. "These should work. Hoodie's oversized, but I know that's how you like it. Or are you not into that anymore?"

"No, no. I very much am still into the oversized hoodie," I said, accepting the pile with a small smile.

He didn't leave right away. He stood in the doorway for a second, rubbing the back of his neck like he was working up to something.

"I'm really glad you decided to stay," he said finally, voice quiet.

I looked up.

"If you need anything, seriously, just let me know. Water, food, a different pillow, whatever. Make yourself at home, okay?"

I nodded, feeling something settle behind my ribs. "Thanks, Miles."

"Goodnight, Keira."

"Goodnight."

He left the door cracked a little when he walked away. I stood there for another second, clothes in my arms, heart tapping lightly against my chest, before turning to the bed.

The guest bed was incredibly soft, the kind that sank just enough to make you feel like you were being held.

I was wrapped in a hoodie that smelled faintly of clean laundry and some faded cologne that belonged to Miles. The sweatpants were big, but comfortable, and I'd rolled the waistband twice just to keep them up.

The apartment was quiet, except for the occasional gust of wind rattling faintly against the windowpane. Snow tapped against the glass in steady little bursts, as the storm had settled in for the long haul.

I reached for my phone on the nightstand. Two unread texts from Jess.

> Jess: Hey. You good? That blizzard's no joke.
>
> Jess: Did the hotel let you extend your stay? I tried calling them to set it up for you but their phone lines were down.

I stared at the screen for a moment before typing.

> Me: Hey. I'm okay, I promise. The hotel's a mess, so I had to figure out something else.
>
> It's... kind of a long story. I'll explain everything soon.

Then, after a second thought, I added:

> Me: I really need to talk to you when all this settles.

She responded almost immediately.

> Jess: Girl. The vagueness is not helping. But fine. I trust you. Just don't go off the grid.
>
> Me: I won't. You'll be the first person I call when I can think.
>
> Jess: Okay. Be safe. And seriously, call me when you can.

I locked my phone and set it back down on the nightstand, then rolled onto my back, staring at the ceiling for a while as the storm whispered against the windows.

So much for a quiet book tour.

I let out a slow breath.

This wasn't how today was supposed to go.

I was supposed to be back at the hotel by now, packing for New York, setting alarms, reviewing my itinerary. Instead, I was snowed in. At my childhood best friend's apartment.

Wearing his clothes. Lying in his guest bed.

It should've felt surreal. Or complicated. Or wrong.

But it didn't.

It felt easy. I couldn't remember the last time I'd felt this at peace. I was cozy and warm and safe in so many aspects of the word.

I stared up at the ceiling and let the silence fill the room.

How did we end up here?

Five years of no contact. Five years of wondering how he was, if he ever thought about me, and now suddenly, we were breathing the same air again. Sharing the same space again.

Like the space between us had always been temporary.

I rolled onto my side, pulling the blanket up to my chin.

I spent all that time trying to forget how much I loved him.

And now, lying here in the warmth of his home, wrapped in his clothes, I realized I never really stopped.

MILES

THEN — AGE 16

PORTLAND, MAINE

I still remember the night she showed up at my door.

It was August, and the heat from the day was still thick in the air even though it was well past one a.m.

A box fan rattled in the corner, pushing the same humid air around the room. I'd fallen asleep on top of the sheets in nothing but gym shorts, my phone face down and quiet on the nightstand.

Suddenly, I heard a small buzz.

Once. Then again.

"Are you awake?"

Then, a second message.

"I'm outside."

I didn't even think twice. I stumbled toward the window, the concrete floor cold under my feet. When I pulled back the curtain, she was crouched there with her hood up, hair sticking to her cheeks, eyes wide and red rimmed in the glow of the porch light.

Keira.

I popped the screen and pushed the window up as quietly as I could. She didn't say anything, she just climbed through like she'd had a dozen times before. She landed on the rug with a soft thud, brushing dirt off her knees.

"Hey," I said, voice low. "Are you okay?"

She didn't answer right away. She just stood there, breathing hard like she'd been walking fast, or maybe holding it together too long.

"It's just my mom, as usual. She told me to get out," she said. Her voice was thin and flat. "So I did."

"Shit. I'm sorry, Keira," I said.

She stayed quiet, and that's how I knew she was feeling something deep. She never went quiet.

"You can have the bed," I offered, already reaching for the blanket I kept at the foot of it.

"I'll crash on the couch."

"No." Her voice was immediate but tired. "I didn't come here to take over your room, I just…I didn't want to be there anymore."

"You're not," I said. "It's fine. I don't mind."

She looked like she might argue again, but then she sat cross-legged on the comforter, her shoulders curled forward like she was holding herself together. Her hands were tugging at the strings of the hoodie in her lap, twisting and untwisting them like she didn't even notice.

I sat down on my desk chair and spun it slightly to face her.

"What happened?"

She shrugged without looking up. "Nothing. Everything. I don't know."

I waited.

"She said I was too dramatic. That I always take things personally. That I act like everything's the end of the world just because someone tells me no." She paused. "All because I asked her if I could apply for the writing retreat in Boston."

I blinked. "Seriously?"

"She said it was a waste of money. That I wasn't thinking practically. That I needed to stop living in this little fantasy where I thought I was special."

That last word cracked something in her. She said it like it still stung.

I swallowed the urge to get angry on her behalf. "You are special."

She gave a soft laugh, bitter and tired. "Yeah, well. Not according to her. She's never believed in me. I can't wait til' college comes and I can finally get out of here."

I leaned forward, elbows on my knees. "Hey."

She looked up, eyes glassy but fierce.

"You are special," I said again. "Whether she sees it or not."

She didn't answer. Just kept twisting the strings of her hoodie, her jaw tight. The silence stretched between us like it was asking to be filled.

"You remember that one time you told me you were gonna live in a lighthouse and write books and never come back to this town? We were thirteen. You said you'd write strictly by candlelight in the winter and eat grilled cheese every day for lunch with tea."

"And never wear shoes. Don't forget that part."

I smiled. "Right. Total feral writer energy."

She let out a soft laugh, but then it faded. "You never laughed at me. Not the way everyone else did."

"Because I believe in you."

That made her pause. Her hands went still in her lap. Then she shifted, slowly curling onto her side. She used her arm as a pillow and pulled the blanket over herself. She looked small on my bed, like she belonged there, right between me and the mattress.

I reached for the spare pillow and throw blanket I had tucked on the lounge chair next to the bed and got ready to settle on the rug. But before I could lie down, she spoke again. "Miles?"

"Yeah?"

"Can you stay up with me? Just for a little while?"

"Yeah," I said, already sitting back on the edge of the bed. "Of course."

She closed her eyes, but her fingers reached toward mine, tentative and tired. I didn't even think; I just took her hand.

We didn't speak again that night.

I lay back against the wall, her hand still in mine, and listened to her breathing until it softened into sleep.

I told myself I'd let go then.

But I never did.

***

NOW

I woke up before I meant to.

It was still dark and just past three in the morning. The apartment was quiet except for the low hum of the heater kicking on and the faint whistle of wind at the windowpanes. I sat up slowly, running a hand over my face.

Then it hit me.

Keira Sullivan was sleeping in my guest room.

That was real. This wasn't a dream.

After all this time, all the silence, all the half-written messages I never sent. She was here. Snowed in with me. Wrapped in one of my old sweatshirts. Breathing the same air.

It was almost like life was giving us a second chance.

I pressed the heels of my hands into my eyes and sat like that for a while, elbows on my knees, just breathing.

So much had changed. We weren't kids anymore. We weren't staying up all night, defying our parents and camping out in my backyard.

She had a life now. A fiancé, even if she barely talked about him.

A book tour. A little shop she owned back east. And I... well, I had my career, my clean apartment, my calendar filled with meetings, designs, and deadlines.

I stood and walked to the kitchen, poured myself a glass of water I didn't really want, and leaned against the counter, listening to the storm still working its way across the city.

Outside, everything was buried under white, but inside, I was a mess.

Because the truth was, part of me never stopped being sixteen. Never stopped remembering how it felt to be the person she ran to when everything else fell apart.

We could have been something if I didn't hesitate. If the timing lined up. If I had just been honest with her. But I let her slip through my fingers long ago.

And now, after all these years, here she was. Right in front of me. And every part of me still wanted to be that person for her.

I decided not to check on her, even though I wanted to, so I just stood in the kitchen longer than I needed to, staring at the hallway like maybe she'd appear there, barefoot and sleepy-eyed, asking for water or company or comfort.

But the door to the guest room stayed shut. And I stayed where I was.

Because I knew myself. I knew that if I knocked, even just to see if she was okay, something would shift. And we weren't ready for that yet.

I knew I wasn't. So I finished my water and went back to bed. I lay there, staring at the ceiling while the wind howled against the glass and the city disappeared beneath the storm.

And even though I didn't hear her voice, or her footsteps, or even the creak of the guest bed settling...I still felt her there.

In the quiet. In the dark. In the part of me that had never really learned how to let her go.

At some point, I must've drifted off.

Because the next thing I knew, I was waking to the soft hum of music playing somewhere outside my door.

For a second, I forgot where I was. Or maybe I just forgot she was here again. This was going to be harder to get used to than I thought.

I pulled on a hoodie and went to the window out of habit. The snow hadn't let up overnight. It blanketed everything outside. All the cars, sidewalks, and even the metal railing leading down to the street.

I'd never seen the city like this before. There wasn't a single soul outside other than those driving the snowplows. The snow was still falling in slow, steady flakes like the whole world had hit pause.

I let out a low whistle. "Damn."

She definitely wasn't going anywhere today.

I rubbed the back of my neck and yawned, then headed down the hall. The music got louder. Fleetwood Mac. Keira's doing, obviously. The sound of a spoon clinking against ceramic echoed softly behind it.

And then I saw her.

She was in the kitchen, totally in her own world. Her hair was pulled up in a loose bun, wisps falling around her face. My hoodie sleeves were pushed to her elbows as she poured hot water over a tea bag. Her phone was propped against the backsplash, the music humming gently in the background. She moved like she'd done this a thousand times before.

I leaned against the doorframe and just watched her for a second, smiling to myself.

There was nothing big about the moment. Nothing dramatic. Just her, in the soft morning light, barefoot on my tile floor, filling the apartment with something I hadn't realized it had been missing.

She looked so much like the version of her I still saw in my head. And yet completely different, too. Older, more sure of herself. More woman than girl, but still her in all the ways that mattered.

I didn't say anything.

Because the truth was, I was a little afraid to break the spell. Because somewhere in the middle of all the silence and the snow and the music, I realized I was falling for her all over again.

She must've sensed me standing there, because just as she turned to reach for the honey, she caught sight of me leaning in the doorway.

"Oh—hey," she said, a little sheepish. "Sorry, I didn't mean to raid your kitchen."

I held up a hand. "Don't let me interrupt."

She gave a small laugh and turned back to the mug. "You were still asleep. I didn't want to wake you, but I figured tea was a safe move."

A small smile pulled at my cheeks. "You found everything okay?"

"Yeah. Hope you don't mind that I poked around a little. The cabinet situation in here is a bit complicated."

"I don't mind," I said. "You're the first person who's ever made tea in my kitchen."

She raised an eyebrow. "That can't be true."

"It is," I said. "Most people just come here for takeout and Netflix."

"Ah," she said, "your usual charm."

"You're welcome to judge me later," I said, reaching for a mug of my own. "Preferably over caffeine." I tapped the buttons on the coffee pot to get it going.

She glanced at me for a moment, just long enough to let me know she was paying attention.

"Honestly, Miles, this place is really nice," she said finally, glancing around. "You did well for yourself. Not that I expected anything less."

"You sound impressed."

"I am."

I caught her staring at the open cabinet. "And you still organize your mugs by size," she said.

I glanced over. "Force of habit."

"You always had oddly specific ones."

I shrugged. "They stack better that way, and you know it."

She didn't say anything at first; she just watched me, her fingers wrapped around one of the mugs.

"I'm happy to see that you're still you," she said quietly.

I cleared my throat and reached for the cabinet behind her.

"You hungry?"

She glanced at me over the rim of her mug. "Depends. What kind of breakfast are we talking about?"

"I've got eggs, bread, maybe some fruit that's still good. If you're lucky, I can even dig up some bacon from somewhere."

"Ooh. Luxury. Honestly, all of that sounds great."

I opened the fridge and gave it a quick scan. "Well, I don't usually cook for guests, but I can be convinced."

She leaned back against the counter, half smiling. "Miles Bennett, are you trying to impress me?"

I pulled out a carton of eggs and closed the door with my hip. "Too early in the morning for games, Sullivan. Let me feed you."

She didn't answer right away, but her smile lingered.

"Alright," she said. "But please try not to burn the toast."

"No promises," I said, turning toward the stove. "But I'll do my best."

Chapter 14

KEIRA

PRESENT DAY

CHICAGO, ILLINOIS

Breakfast had lingered on longer than we expected. The plates were mostly cleared, the kettle had gone cold, and the playlist I had put on earlier was looping back around to the beginning.

Outside, the city had vanished behind white. Not just snow-dusted but completely swallowed. I knew I wouldn't be traveling for quite a while if it kept up like this.

I glanced over at Miles, who had his back to me while he washed the last of the dishes. The t-shirt he was wearing clung to his back in just the right way, outlining the shape of muscles he didn't have in college. Come to think of it, I'd never seen him with any kind of muscle definition, ever.

His shoulders had always been broad, but now they looked solid. The fabric shifted with each bit of movement, the hem lifting slightly to reveal the faint line of skin above his waistband.

It was infuriating how good he looked. And even worse, how natural it still felt to look at him like that.

He glanced over at me and noticed my gawking. "See something you like?" he asked with that charming smirk of his.

I balled up a hand towel and tossed it at him, laughing awkwardly. "Oh, please. Don't flatter yourself."

He caught it effortlessly and laughed it off. "I'm gonna jump in the shower," he said, "shouldn't be long."

I nodded casually, even though I suddenly felt like I was thirteen again and trying not to act weird about being in a boy's house. "Yeah, go ahead. I'll just hang out."

"Back in a bit," he said, heading down the hall.

I watched him go. The door to the bathroom clicked shut a few seconds later, and the apartment settled into stillness. I stood in the middle of the living room with my empty mug in my hands, unsure of what to do next.

I didn't mean to wander.

But my curiosity got the best of me.

There was a framed photo on the bookshelf, hidden between architectural books and an old baseball cap. A family picture, probably a few years old. Miles, his sister, and their parents.

They were at the beach—windblown, sunburned, smiling in that way people do when they're caught off guard and happy.

I ran my fingers lightly along the top of the frame, then moved on.

His apartment was comfortably lived in. A pair of boots sat by the door, and a stack of mail lay neatly on the counter. He had a print of the Chicago skyline hanging near the window, and next to it, a small shelf with a few model buildings and sketches. One of them looked like a cathedral. Another was just a series of lines and curves, but I could tell it had taken hours.

He'd built a life here.

And I hadn't been part of any of it.

I swallowed and turned toward the hallway, where I noticed his bedroom door was cracked open.

I told myself I was just looking for a charger.

That was the excuse I mentally settled on when I found myself pushing open the door at the end of the hall and stepping inside what was very clearly his bedroom.

The bed was neatly made, a sweatshirt was draped over the desk chair, and an open sketchbook lay beside his laptop. A pair of running shoes rested neatly against the wall. The blinds were partially open, letting in the soft blue and white light of the storm still unfolding outside.

I shouldn't have been in there.

But I crossed the room anyway, my heart picking up speed. Not out of fear, but of that warm, weightless flutter that comes when you know you're toeing a line and doing it anyway.

Like I was a kid again and about to get caught somewhere I wasn't supposed to be.

The faint scent of his cologne still lingered in the room. He still wore that same warm, cedarwood scent that I loved. I brushed my fingers along the edge of the desk, eyes trailing over the little things that made it his. Coins in a ceramic bowl. A few old wristbands from concerts. A yellow sticky note with an upcoming appointment of some sort scribbled on it.

I walked by the open closet. It was mostly what you'd expect. Shirts, jackets, and neatly stacked shoeboxes took up most of the space. An umbrella leaned against the corner, forgotten. And that's when I saw it.

A small shoebox on the top shelf.

It wasn't labeled neatly like the others, not marked with brand logos or dates. Just a single word was scrawled across the side in black marker: Keira.

My breath caught.

I stared at it, pulse thudding behind my ribs. For a second, I didn't move. I didn't know what I expected to find inside. Maybe a letter or a photo, some tiny part of me he hadn't let go of. Something he'd kept when I hadn't even realized there was anything worth keeping.

I reached up on instinct, fingers just brushing the corner of the lid when my phone rang.

The sharp buzz made me jump. I yanked my hand back like I'd been burned, stepping away from the closet as if someone had just shouted my name from across the room.

I pulled the phone from my pocket.

Dylan.

The name on the screen sent a different kind of flutter through me.

I stepped out of Miles' room and headed for the living room, all the while my thumb hovering over the green icon. I sighed and answered.

"Hey," I said quietly, steadying my voice. "What's going on?"

There was a quiet beat, and then Dylan's voice came through. "Babe, I've been trying to get a hold of you all morning," he said. "Is everything okay?"

"Yeah, of course, I'm really sorry. I didn't hear it ring before."

"I figured you'd be holed up somewhere. Did they cancel the rest of your tour?"

"Not officially," I said, moving to sit on the edge of the couch. "But everything's paused for now. Chicago's pretty much buried, so I think I'm gonna be stuck here a few more days."

"Damn, that's awful. Do you know when you'll be able to leave?"

I rubbed a hand across my temple. "No idea. It's not just flights, it's the roads, too. Everything's shut down."

"Jesus." He let out a breath. "Where did you end up staying? Did Jess find you another place?"

I hesitated for a second too long. Here we go. "Actually, I'm at a friend's place."

"A friend? In Chicago?"

"Yeah."

Another pause. "I didn't even know you knew anyone in Chicago. Is it someone I know?"

I swallowed. "No. It's actually an old friend of mine from Portland who moved here a few years ago."

"An old friend? Is this friend a guy?"

"Dylan," I said quickly, forcing calm into my voice. "I'm fine. He's just helping me out so I'm not stuck alone in a hotel. It's not a big deal."

He didn't say anything for a few seconds. When he finally did, his voice was tight. "Right. Not a big deal. My fiancé is staying at some random guy's house, but it's not a big deal."

I stood and walked toward the window, needing to move. "He's not a random guy," I said, my voice suddenly sounding defensive. I took a breath to calm myself down. "Dylan, please. Just trust me. There is nothing going on. I don't know how long I'll be stuck here. But hopefully not more than a day or two."

"Well, you didn't mention that you knew anyone there who could possibly give you a place to stay. I would've liked to be in the loop on that."

"I didn't know last night. Not initially," I said, turning from the window. "Everything happened so fast. There weren't a lot of options, and it was getting late by the time we figured it all out."

"You could've called."

"I know. You're right, and I'm sorry, but why are you being like this?" Another silence.

"I'm just trying to understand what's going on," he said quietly. "You've been acting so different lately. I may not have said much about it, but I notice things, Keira."

I blinked. "Different how?"

"I don't know. Distant, I guess. I just…I want to be there for you. But lately it feels like you're a thousand miles away even when we're standing right next to each other."

His words landed harder than I expected. Maybe because they weren't totally wrong.

I pressed my fingers to my forehead and closed my eyes. "I'm tired. That's all. It's been a long week."

"I miss you," he said. "I want to fix whatever this is. I'm not happy about this situation, but I will trust you, of course."

And just like that, I felt it again. That slow, aching pull of guilt. Of obligation. Of saying the right thing instead of the real one.

"Thank you for trusting me," I said. "I miss you too."

"Well, keep me updated, please. We can talk more about this when you get home. I love you."

"I love you too."

I clicked off my phone and tossed it onto the rug in front of me. The room was quiet. Still warm from the morning, but the silence had a different texture now. It was heavier.

I sank back against the couch cushions, pulling the throw blanket a little tighter around my legs. Outside, the world had disappeared behind a thick curtain of snow. The buildings across the street were blurred at the edges, and the cars parked below had all but vanished under white.

I stared out at it, letting the silence fill every part of me that Dylan's voice hadn't reached.

He hadn't done anything wrong. He cared. He wanted to help. But everything between us felt like it had been stretched too far for too long. Even his words—I miss you, I want to fix this—had started to feel like phrases we were supposed to say instead of things we actually meant. I didn't know when that started. I just knew I couldn't pretend it wasn't happening anymore.

Sometimes I felt like it was all me. Like I was sabotaging something good, but the real question was: Even though something is good, was it good for me?

I brought my knees up and rested my chin, closed my eyes, and breathed deeply, counting slowly in my head. I was okay. I was warm. I was safe.

I was just somewhere I never expected to be.

I heard the bathroom door open a moment before he appeared.

His footsteps were quiet against the hardwood, and when I looked up, he was standing in the doorway to the living room, towel slung around his neck. He'd changed into a clean t-shirt and joggers; his hair was still damp from the shower and curled at the edges, and a bead of water trailed from his neck down to the collar of his shirt.

The fabric clung just enough to show the lines of his chest, and the joggers sat low on his hips in a way that made it hard to look away. He looked so good in a completely effortless kind of way, and somehow that made it worse.

His eyes landed on me right away.

"You okay?" he asked, ever observant.

I gave him the best smile I could muster, tucking my legs in tighter beneath the blanket. "Yeah. I'm just getting a little worried. The storm's really coming down."

He looked at me for a second longer, like he was trying to read between the lines. Then he nodded slowly. "Yeah. It's insane."

He crossed the room and sat down at the opposite end of the couch, leaving a comfortable space between us.

"Thanks for letting me stay," I said quietly. "I know it wasn't the plan."

"You kidding?" He smiled faintly. "Best weather-related surprise I've had in years. Years. I still can't believe it's been that long.

I let out a small laugh, more breath than sound.

He leaned his head back against the couch, looking toward the window. "I don't think I've ever seen this much snow in the city. I'm not gonna lie, though, it's nice to have a break from work."

"Yeah," I said. "I know what you mean."

We sat there in the quiet, the soft hum of the radiator filling the space between us.

He turned to me again. "You sure you're alright?"

I nodded. "Just tired. It's been a long twenty-four hours."

I don't know how many times I'd use the tired excuse, but the word was starting to give me a migraine.

He didn't push. Just gave a small, understanding nod and looked away again.

The silence between us lingered, thick with everything unsaid. I wanted to ask what was on his mind, to spill everything I'd been holding back, but the words caught in my throat.

So instead, I curled up, rested my head against the couch cushion, and said quietly, "This is nice."

He glanced over at me, his voice just as soft. "I'm glad you think so."

He got up after a moment and stood in front of the bookshelf, then muttered, "I've been meaning to fix this for months." He crouched down and started pulling books off the shelves.

I followed him to the floor, tucking my legs under me as he passed me a stack. "Alphabetical?" I asked, raising an eyebrow. "Or some random system that only makes sense to you?"

He smirked. "Let's not pretend I've ever alphabetized anything in my life. We'll go with instinct."

We spent the rest of the morning like that; books scattered around us, coffee mugs within reach, the snow falling heavy outside the window. We talked about the ones we loved, the ones we never finished, the ones we only bought because of the cover art. He handed me a copy of *East of Eden* and said it wrecked him the first time he read it. I gave him *The Secret History* from my stack and told him that it was in my top five favorite reads.

"Of course it is," he said with a grin, flipping it over. "Dark academia and morally questionable characters? That tracks."

I laughed and nudged his shoulder. "Says the man who owns three copies of *The Road*." He didn't deny it. Just smiled and passed me another book.

I loved that literature was something we shared. I'd always carried that love with me, even as a kid, while his came later. Something that he grew into over time. Eventually, we started trading books, swapping recommendations, and texting each other lines we couldn't stop thinking about.

Before I realized it, the morning had slipped into early afternoon. Miles glanced over at me.

"You hungry?" he asked.

I nodded, shifting the blanket off my lap. "Starving, actually."

"I've got stuff for a couple of grilled cheeses and tomato soup. It's basic, but—"

"It's perfect, you know better than anyone that I love a good grilled cheese," I said before he could finish.

That earned a small smile from him, the kind that eased the tension in his face just a little.

"Alright then. Give me ten minutes to wow you."

I followed him into the kitchen and perched on one of the stools at the island as he pulled out the bread, cheese, and a can of soup from the pantry. He moved around the kitchen comfortably, and it suddenly felt like we were back in our old apartment, just going about the day like we used to.

As he poured the soup into a pot, he glanced over his shoulder. "You remember that spur-of-the-moment trip up to the mountain we took?"

I laughed. "You mean the one where I ended up cracking my brand new snowboard, and you sprained your wrist?"

"Exactly. Great times."

I shook my head, smiling. "What about it?"

"We split this order at the lodge. Buffalo chicken strips and a Caesar salad. Do you remember?"

"Oh my God, yes. We were freezing and starving, and that food tasted like the best thing in the world."

He grinned to himself as he stirred the soup. "I swear I've been chasing that exact meal ever since. Nothing ever hits the same."

"It was probably just the hunger. And the hypothermia."

"Speak for yourself. I've got a culinary void that's never been filled."

The smell of butter and melting cheese filled the kitchen. It felt like a memory itself, warm and simple. He plated everything and slid one of the bowls in front of me, along with a sandwich cut diagonally.

"You remembered," I said, a little surprised.

He shrugged. "Of course I did. It's also the only correct way to eat one of these."

His blue eyes met mine, and something about the way he looked at me made my stomach flip. I glanced down, a quiet smile tugging at my lips before I could stop it.

We sat and ate in companionable silence for a while as the wind howled outside, the snow pressing up heavily against the windows. I didn't realize how hungry I was until halfway through the sandwich.

"This is really good," I said, mouth full.

Miles gave me a mock serious nod. "I told you. Culinary excellence."

I watched him for a second longer than I meant to. The curve of his mouth when he smiled. The way his eyes looked softer now. There were pieces of him I hadn't seen in years, and maybe pieces I'd never seen at all.

I looked down at my plate and took another bite, trying not to think too hard about the fact that I didn't want this day to end.

The afternoon turned into evening too quickly. I was still curled into the corner of the couch, except this time with a cup of tea, when Miles came back from the hall closet holding a cardboard box with a proud grin spread across his face.

"Look what I found."

I raised a brow. "Oh God, please don't say Monopoly. I don't think I could deal with your cheating tonight."

"Worse," he said, lifting the lid. "Scrabble."

I let out a dramatic groan. "Don't think I don't remember that you're impossible to play against. You make up fake words and gaslight me into believing they're real."

"They're not fake. I just have range."

I laughed and set my mug down, already pulling my legs under me to face him. "Fine. But I'm watching you."

He raised both hands in mock surrender. "Scout's honor."

We sat on the living room floor, the board between us, the sound of one of my vintage playlists humming low from the Bluetooth speaker behind us.

It felt a little like time travel back to nights when we were kids and snowed in at one of our parents' houses, still high on energy from a movie marathon.

It didn't take long for the competitiveness to come out. I caught him trying to pass off "chumbled" as a verb.

"Miles, that's not a word."

He didn't even flinch. "It's British slang."

"For what?"

"For...well, I don't really remember, but I know it's a word! I saw it one time somewhere."

I stared him down. "I know that's not in the dictionary."

"You don't know that."

I rolled my eyes and made him lose his turn. "I'm a writer, of course I do."

A few moves later, I laid down the word *loved*. I swear I didn't plan it. It was the last of my tiles, and just so happened to work out that way. Miles glanced at it, then at me, but didn't say anything. He added "late" to the top corner of the board and leaned back, stretching.

"You win," he said.

I blinked. "We're not done."

"I'm retiring before you humiliate me."

I smiled, watching him stand to gather the tiles. "You're such a sore loser."

"And you're still just as competitive."

As we were cleaning up, a thought very clearly crossed his mind. "You know, I think I still have our yearbook somewhere."

I looked up. "Seriously?"

He was already halfway down the hall. I loved seeing him like this. All giddy like a teenager again. When he came back a minute later, he was holding a dusty navy blue hardcover with silver foil lettering and a cracked spine. I took it gently when he handed it over and sat cross-legged on the couch.

"God," I muttered, flipping through. "We thought we were so cool."

"We weren't," he said, flopping down beside me. "We really weren't."

We flipped pages together, laughing at awkward prom photos and club pages with names I barely remembered. He pointed out our math teacher, who'd always worn mismatched socks, and I found a picture of him from the spring theater production behind a curtain, holding a light fixture.

And then I found us.

A photo from the senior trip to Acadia National Park. I was wearing a hoodie three sizes too big, my hair a mess. Miles had his arm slung casually over my shoulders, both of us squinting into the sun. We looked so young, so careless. So blissfully unaware of how difficult life could be.

I didn't say anything at first. I just stared.

He leaned closer, our knees brushing. "Feels like another lifetime."

"It kind of was," I said, my voice softer than I meant it to be.

For a second, the only sound in the room was the wind outside. My fingers lingered on the page, tracing the edge of the image like I was afraid it might disappear if I blinked.

I could feel tears threatening to spill if I looked any longer. I closed the book gently and handed it back to him.

"I think I've had enough nostalgia for one day."

Miles nodded, but he didn't look away. Just studied me for a moment like he was trying to figure something out.

We didn't talk much after that. The music kept playing. The snow kept falling.

Eventually, we both drifted back to the couch with him at one end, me at the other. I curled up beneath the throw blanket, watching the flicker of the muted TV screen. Not really watching.

He yawned and leaned his head back against the cushion, eyes slipping closed.

Neither of us said it, but we weren't pretending anymore. This day, the way we could just fall so easily back into it. These weren't just old memories.

It was something else.

We were waking back up.

Chapter 15

MILES

❄

PRESENT DAY

CHICAGO, ILLINOIS

The room was dark except for the flicker of the TV screen, its blue light casting soft shadows across the walls. I blinked awake slowly, disoriented for a second. My neck ached from how I was slumped, my arm pinned awkwardly behind a pillow.

I felt a shift, looked down, and froze. Keira had at some point fallen asleep on my lap, curled on her side so naturally, like she belonged there. Her knees were tucked up close, one hand cradled beneath her cheek, the other resting loosely on the blanket we must've pulled over us at some point. Her mouth was parted slightly, her breathing soft and even.

It had been years since I'd seen her sleep like that, and somehow she looked exactly the same.

I sat up carefully and glanced at the clock on my phone. 11:47 p.m. The house was quiet, the storm outside still pressing rough against the windows, though the wind seemed like it was finally starting to die down.

I turned the volume on the TV down, just enough to keep it from waking her, then I looked back.

God.

Even in sleep, she looked like the version of herself I hadn't realized I'd been missing. She seemed completely at ease, like time had finally given something back. Her hair had fallen forward, messier now, a few strands brushing against her mouth.

I didn't think. I just reached out and tucked one gently behind her ear, letting my fingers linger just a second too long.

Thankfully, she didn't stir.

Eventually, I pushed myself up with a quiet exhale and slipped one arm under her knees and the other beneath her back. She stirred just a little, murmuring something I couldn't catch. Her head fell lightly against my shoulder.

Carrying her like that felt too familiar. The way she naturally leaned into me was trusting, like her body remembered even if her mind wouldn't let her. I tried not to read too much into it. I tried not to feel anything at all, but I just couldn't help it.

I pushed open the door to the guest room with my foot and laid her gently down on the bed, pulling the blanket up over her shoulders. She turned onto her side without waking, fingers curling beneath her chin.

I stood there for a beat too long, taking in the shape of her in the quiet. The curve of her shoulder beneath the blanket, the way her hair fell over her face, the impossibly unfair fact that after all this time, I still wanted to memorize her.

"Goodnight, Keira," I said softly, though she couldn't hear me.

And then I turned off the light and closed the door behind me.

***

I woke to a faint gray light outside the window. For a minute, I didn't move; I just listened to the quiet. No traffic, no footsteps on the sidewalk, no city noise at all. The storm hadn't stopped, but it had softened. Everything outside was still covered in deep, untouched snow.

My back was sore from the couch, but I expected as much. I pushed the blanket off and sat up slowly, rubbing my face with both hands. Coffee was the first thought that popped into my mind.

In the kitchen, I started a kettle and leaned on the counter. I kept thinking about last night. About how easily it had all slipped back into something familiar. And if I was being completely honest, that scared the absolute shit out of me.

I heard her before I saw her, the little shuffle of feet across the hallway floor. I hadn't meant to stare when she walked in, but it sort of just happened. She looked half-asleep and flushed from warmth, her hair twisted up in a lazy knot. That sweatshirt of mine hit her mid-thigh, the sleeves too long, her fingers barely poking out.

It wasn't just that she looked good. She always had. It was seeing her like that, in my space, in something that belonged to me. I, somehow, managed to manifest the version of the life I wanted—her standing in front of me, barefoot on my kitchen tile, just like this.

It threw me more than I wanted to admit.

So I looked away. Focused on the mugs. The kettle. Anything else.

Because wanting her had never been the hard part.

It was everything that came after.

Her eyes met mine as she walked into the kitchen, still a little squinty from sleep.

"How did I end up in bed last night?" she asked, her voice low and rough from having just woken.

I grabbed two mugs from the cabinet. "You fell asleep on the couch, so I carried you to bed."

She raised an eyebrow. "Seriously?"

I poured hot water into a mug and passed it to her. "You were completely out. Figured it was better than letting you wake up sore."

She smiled, almost to herself. "That's really considerate."

"You're welcome," I said, sipping my coffee.

She stayed quiet for a second, eyes on the window, her fingers curled loosely around the mug. Then her voice dropped a little, softer than before.

"You know, I used to try and picture you," she said. "Where you were living. What your apartment looked like."

I glanced at her, but she didn't look back. Just kept her focus on the steam rising from her cup like she wasn't sure she should've said it out loud.

"You did?" I asked, my voice quieter now.

She nodded. "For a while. It was easier to imagine it all, since I didn't really have a choice other than that."

I swallowed hard. My stomach twisted, and I knew it was only a matter of time until we got to this conversation. Her words managed to find the part of me that still hadn't forgiven myself.

"I wanted to call," I said, and the words felt clumsy leaving my mouth. "I thought about it. I just…didn't know how to fix it without making it worse."

Her eyes flicked to mine then, sharp and searching. Not angry, but not unreadable either.

There was clear disappointment there.

"That's the thing. There was nothing to fix, Miles."

I was about to respond, something low building in my chest, but her phone lit up just then on the counter.

She looked down, and her expression dimmed.

"Sorry," she said quietly, already stepping away. "I have to take this."

I watched her disappear down the hall, the sound of her voice drifting as she headed into the bedroom.

I didn't purposefully try to eavesdrop. I was just standing in the kitchen, rinsing out my mug, trying to give her space. But the place wasn't that big, and when her voice carried down the hallway, I froze.

"Yes, I'm still here. I told you, there weren't many options," she was saying. "It's not like I planned for the blizzard."

Her voice was calm but tired, like it had already run through this conversation before.

"I didn't think you'd still be hung up on it," she added. "You said it was fine yesterday."

A pause. I could hear her pacing, the soft footsteps on the wood floor of the guest room.

She always paced when she was anxious, like movement could keep her from unraveling.

"No, of course I'm not hiding anything," she said. "I just didn't think it was worth going over again."

Another long silence. I didn't need to hear the other end of the call to know what was being said. I could feel it in her voice, in the way it kept thinning out like she was holding her breath between words.

"I'll be back when I can," she said finally. "That hasn't changed."

Her tone was quieter now. Worn out. "No, I don't know yet. I haven't had time to figure it all out. I'm doing the best I can."

She didn't say goodbye when she hung up. Just the soft click of the call ending, then nothing. I stepped back from the sink and reached for my coffee like I hadn't just heard the whole thing. Like I wasn't standing there trying to decide whether I felt more furious or sad on her behalf.

When she walked back into the kitchen, she had that look again. The one she always got when she was trying not to let anyone see what she was feeling. She gave me a small, polite smile like nothing had happened. Like I hadn't just heard her defend herself to someone who was supposed to love her.

"You alright?" I asked, keeping my voice light.

She nodded without hesitation, but it didn't look convincing. "Yeah. Just Dylan checking in. It's fine."

I didn't push. I could tell she didn't want me to.

So instead I nodded toward the window. "Snow's still coming down, but it's lighter than earlier. Think we're still stuck in for a while, though."

She followed my gaze and gave a small nod. "Looks like it."

We both stood there for a beat too long. Her tea sat untouched now. And all I could think about was how close she felt last night, and how far she seemed again this morning.

The rest of the morning passed quietly. Keira took a few calls from her agent, someone from the publishing house, and what sounded like a friend named Jess who kept making her laugh in that dry, sarcastic way. I stayed in the background for most of it, cleaning up, flipping through a book I had started a few days ago, and folding the throw blankets we'd used from the night before.

It wasn't awkward exactly, but there was a distance between us again. Somewhere between our last conversation and Dylan's phone call, things felt fragile.

Every now and then, she'd look over at me with this unreadable expression, like she was trying to decide what to say. And then she wouldn't say anything at all.

Around noon, I offered to make lunch. She didn't argue. We sat at the table with grilled cheese again and leftover tomato soup between us, the sound of the wind low against the windows. She thanked me for the food and tossed a smile my way, but it didn't quite meet her eyes.

Still, something started to loosen again as the afternoon stretched on. We passed the time slowly. She found an old deck of cards in a drawer, and we played a half-hearted game of rummy while the heater hummed and the snow piled up along the window ledges. I let her win. She pretended not to notice.

Later, she sat curled in the corner of the couch with her legs tucked under her and a book cracked open on her lap. I sat nearby, sort of reading, but mostly watching the way her lips moved slightly when she read silently to herself.

By six, the wind turned quiet. I glanced out the window, arms crossed loosely over my chest. The snowfall was lighter now, and for the first time all day, the world outside didn't look like something to be afraid of. It looked inviting.

"Looks like we survived the worst of it."

Keira looked up from the couch where she'd been reading, one leg still tucked under her.

"Think they'll lift the travel ban?"

I shrugged. "Maybe tomorrow. For now, though…" I turned back toward her with a small grin. "Wanna go outside?"

She blinked. "Outside?"

I nodded. "Just for a little bit. Get some air. We've been cooped up the last two days."

She hesitated for a moment, then set the book down and stretched her arms overhead. "Alright. Why not?"

We both layered up with coats, scarves, and gloves we found in the hall closet. I handed her a knit beanie I barely wore anymore, and she pulled it on with a laugh.

"You've had this since high school," she said, adjusting it over her ears.

"Yeah, I guess I have a hard time letting go of things."

I hadn't thought about what I said until the words already left my mouth. Thankfully, she didn't seem to notice.

The streets were quiet when we stepped outside, blanketed in untouched snow that came up to our knees in certain spots. The city felt muffled and unfamiliar, like we were the only ones left in the world. The only sound was the soft crunch beneath our boots and the occasional flap of wind against the buildings.

Keira looked around slowly, cheeks pink from the cold, eyes wide. "It's beautiful."

I watched her as she stared out into the snowy night, the glow from the street lamp above us lighting her face just enough to make my breath catch. I couldn't take my eyes off her.

"Yeah," I said quietly. "It really is."

We walked for a few blocks, and at one point, she bent down, scooped up a handful of snow, and lobbed it straight at me, catching my shoulder.

I stared at her. "Really?"

She smirked. "Sorry, I couldn't help myself."

I bent down and packed one quickly. "Alright. Game on. Just know, this will end poorly for you."

We ended up in a full snowball fight on the edge of a small neighborhood park, laughing breathlessly, slipping over patches of hidden ice, calling each other names like we were kids again. For the first time in weeks, maybe even months, my life felt simple.

She ducked behind a bench for cover, breathless with laughter. "Surrender, Bennett!"

"Only if you do, Sullivan!" I shouted back, tossing another one in her direction.

She popped up, laughing so hard she couldn't throw straight, and it stirred up something deep inside of me. It was like seeing her again for the first time. Not the Keira I'd been tiptoeing around the last few hours, but the one I'd known my whole life. Unfiltered and full of light.

**

THEN — AGE 13

CAMP RUSHWOOD, SEBAGO, MAINE

It was way too hot to do anything. Keira had found me out by the docks and begged me to go sneak a canoe out with her before the dinner bell rang. We weren't technically supposed to go out without a counselor, but Keira didn't care about rules, and neither did I.

The lake felt like bathwater. Warm and murky and greenish, with bugs skimming across the top, the sound of other campers yelling from the shore.

We paddled out slow, Keira in front and me in back. She talked the whole way down the trail about how gross the camp food had been that day, about a spider she found in the shower, about how she was going to sneak out that night to steal brownies from the kitchen.

I didn't say much. I never really did when she was talking like that. I just liked listening to her.

We stopped close to the island in the middle of the lake and let our canoe float there for a while. Keira sat cross-legged at the front of the canoe, squinting into the sun, her hair in two loose braids with pieces falling out around her face. She dipped her hand into the water, dragging it through as we drifted.

There were lily pads everywhere, flat and green and floating on top of the water like little frisbees. Keira leaned over the side and tried to pull off one of the flowers with no luck.

I couldn't help but laugh as she struggled.

"You think that's funny? I dare you to touch one," she said, nodding toward the lily pads.

"They're just plants," I said.

"Exactly." She grinned. "So then do it!"

I reached down and grabbed a lily pad by the stem, lifting it like a trophy. She burst out laughing.

"Oh my God," she said, "you actually did it."

"You dared me!" I said, already smiling.

She plucked one that had been bigger than mine and tossed it at me. The underside of the pad unexpectedly stuck to my arm. I took my hand and wiped off as much of the slime as I could before deciding this meant war.

"Okay," I warned. "You started this."

"Bring it on, Bennett."

I lunged forward and swatted her arm with my lily pad like it was a sword. She shrieked and grabbed another, and the next thing I knew, lily pads were flying everywhere.

We ended up both kneeling in the boat, covered in soggy bits of lake plants and laughing so hard I got a stitch in my side.

The canoe rocked with every movement, but somehow, we didn't flip. I kind of wished we had. It would've been the perfect ending to the dumbest, best battle ever.

"Okay, okay. Truce!" she yelled through giggles, holding her hands up, lily pads drooping from each one.

I fell back onto my heels, breathless. She sat down too, her legs dangling over the edge of the boat. We were soaked and covered in bits of green. I remember watching a drop of water slide down her cheek and disappear under her chin, and thinking how pretty she looked. Even with lily pad slime all over her.

Neither of us said anything for a while. The sun was just starting to go down behind the trees, and in the distance, the dinner bell started to ring. I remember her kicking her feet, like she couldn't sit still.

I looked at her, then glanced away before she could notice. Her nose was a little sunburned, freckles scattered across it, as they always did in the summer. A piece of her hair had come loose, curling against her cheek, and she smelled like sunscreen.

I didn't really get why, but my stomach did this weird little flip when she smiled at me.

"You're not bad company, Bennett," she said, and that was the nicest thing she'd ever told me, so I just shrugged like it was no big deal.

But I knew I'd remember it for the rest of my life.

***

NOW

"You're seriously the worst at this," she called, already backing away, her boots crunching through the untouched snow like it was a challenge.

"Oh, is that right?" I shouted, ducking to grab a handful of snow. "You want to test that?"

She shrieked and turned to run, her laugh echoing across the quiet street. I chased after her, slipping slightly but keeping pace, the freezing air burning in my lungs, but it didn't bother me.

She looked back over her shoulder, her eyes bright and cheeks flushed, and for a second, I couldn't breathe.

"Okay, okay!" she said, nearly tripping over a snowbank. "I surrender!"

"Nope," I said, grinning. "Too late for that."

I caught up to her near the edge of the park. My arms went around her waist instinctively as I grabbed her, and we tumbled into the snow together.

It wasn't graceful at all. We fell while laughing wildly on our way down. I landed first, flat on my back, and she landed right on top of me, her coat pressed to mine, her breath hot against the cold.

We laughed until we were both out of breath, the kind of laugh that left your cheeks sore. When the quiet settled in, she didn't move from on top of me. I reached out and brushed a loose strand of hair from her face and tucked it gently behind her ear, my hand slower to fall away than it should've been.

She didn't pull away. Her eyes found mine, searching, and the smile she'd been wearing faded into something unspoken. Her lips parted like she wanted to say something, but the words didn't come.

I watched her closely. Watched every flicker of hesitation, every beat of conflict cross her face, and for the first time in five years, I felt it. And I knew she felt it too. That pull. That ache. That stupid, impossible hope still curled somewhere deep in both of us. The gray sky blurred around the edges of my vision, and all I could see was her.

My hands slid up along her hips, then along the curve of her back, just gently enough, and I felt her breath hitch.

She leaned in a little. Just enough to blur the line. My heart knocked hard against my ribs, and still I didn't move. I wanted to. God, I wanted to. I wanted to close the gap, tilt my head, and taste the years we'd lost. But I didn't.

I waited for her.

Her eyes dropped to my mouth. Her fingers tightened just slightly where they rested over my heart.

"I—" she started.

But she didn't finish.

Because just then, a loud voice cracked across the quiet, "Hey! You two okay over there?"

We both jerked apart, scrambling to sit up as a police cruiser rolled to a stop at the edge of the road. A middle-aged cop leaned out the window, looking more cold than concerned.

"City's under curfew," he said, voice muffled behind a scarf. "You're not supposed to be out unless it's essential. Roads are still dangerous."

"Sorry," I called back. "We were just heading back."

Keira brushed snow off her coat, cheeks burning now for a different reason. "Right," she said quickly. "Sorry for the trouble!"

The cop nodded once and drove off slowly. I glanced at her, trying not to smile. She wouldn't meet my eyes.

We started walking again, side by side, the silence between us different now. I kept my hands in my pockets and tried not to think too hard about how close we'd just been.

Tomorrow, I told myself.

Maybe tomorrow.

Chapter 16

KEIRA

PRESENT DAY

CHICAGO, ILLINOIS

I kept replaying it in my head.

The second our faces got too close. The way his breath hitched. The way mine did too. And the quiet, heavy pause between us where everything else disappeared, until reality came crashing back in the form of a patrol car and a voice telling us it was time to head home.

But the moment followed us. It sat with me through the silence. Stood beside me on the walk home. Followed me into the kitchen, into the corners of my thoughts, into the way I avoided looking at him now.

I almost kissed him.

That was the part I couldn't excuse away. I had wanted it. I wanted to fall into something familiar and warm and comfortable. I'd told myself this trip was about the book, the tour, the schedule. But standing in the snow with him, inches apart, I hadn't been thinking about any of that. Just him.

And then came the guilt. Swift and loud and pulsing in my chest like a warning bell.

I was engaged.

I had someone waiting for me to come home. Someone who'd put a ring on my finger and made plans and talked about mortgages and timelines. Someone who loved me in a quiet, steady way that was supposed to be enough.

And maybe it was. Or maybe I was just trying to believe it still was, even when every second with Miles chipped away at the life I had created. I wasn't being fair to Dylan. He deserved better, someone who could love him completely. It couldn't just be about what was fair to me. It had to be about what was fair to him too.

I didn't know what I felt anymore.

By now, it was after seven, and I stood in front of the open fridge fiddling with anything in there I could find. Really, I just needed to look busy.

"So, we've got a jar of tomato sauce and a box of spaghetti," I said, keeping my voice even.

Miles stood near the doorway, hands in his pockets. "Yeah, that's fine. Want me to get it going?"

"I've got it."

I grabbed the pots and a couple of plates and set the stove on high. The silence settled in again. It was comfortable and tense all at once. Like we were both pretending everything was normal, but every movement felt like we were both walking on eggshells.

He moved beside me, grabbing silverware from the drawer. "You want water or something?"

"Water's good."

We didn't look at each other. The sounds of the kitchen filled in the gaps: water running, the microwave humming, the soft clink of cutlery. I was so incredibly aware of him in that moment.

When he handed me my plate, our fingers brushed. I looked up, and he looked back, but neither of us said anything. I forced a smile, small and automatic.

"Thanks," I said.

He nodded straight-faced. "No problem."

Ugh, every second of this was killing me.

We took our plates to the living room and sat on the couch with a little more space between us than earlier. I tried not to overthink it. I tried not to remember how close we'd been in the snow or how badly I'd wanted him to close the distance. I focused on the food.

The couch. The flicker of shadows from the streetlights outside.

After a few bites, he cleared his throat. "So…the cop kind of killed the moment, huh?"

I glanced at him, surprised that he'd brought it up. "You think there was a moment?"

He gave a soft shrug. "I don't know. Felt like one."

I stared down at my plate, knowing full well there was a moment. "Maybe."

What the hell game am I trying to play? Just be honest with him!

Just then, the lights flickered once above us, then again.

I froze, my fork halfway to my mouth. Across from me, Miles paused too.

"You pay your electric bill?" I asked lightly, trying to joke.

That got him to crack a smile. "Always," he said. "But the grid's probably overloaded. Everyone's inside, cranking the heat."

A second later, everything cut out. The lights. The hum of the fridge. Even the soft buzz from the baseboard heater. Gone. Just like that.

"Well," I said into the sudden quiet. "That answers that."

Miles stood, setting his plate aside. "I've got candles. Stay where you are, and I'll grab them."

"Just be careful," I called to him somewhere in the dark.

My eyes started to adjust, and when he came back, he was

carrying a mismatched armful of candles. Thick white ones, tea lights in little tins, and a few short glass jars that looked like they'd been shoved to the back of a cabinet and forgotten about.

We lit them one by one. It was strangely comforting how calm he was through it all. I followed his lead, placing the flickering lights around the living room until the space glowed in soft, uneven gold. Seeing how beautiful and peaceful it looked made something warm bloom inside the center of my chest.

We didn't say much as we cleaned up dinner and moved to the floor with extra blankets. It was getting colder now without the heat. I pulled my legs under me and tucked the ends of a blanket around my shoulders.

"This is kind of nice," I said, reaching for my water.

Miles nodded. "I've had worse nights."

The quiet stretched between us, soft and steady, like we were both afraid to break it. Only the faint clink of glass or the rustle of a blanket filled the space. Until, at last, his voice cut through the stillness.

"Can I ask you something?" he said.

I looked up. "Sure."

"Are you happy?" he asked. "With him?"

I blinked. "That's not a simple question."

He looked around the room, holding his arms out. "I've clearly got time."

I looked down at the floor, tracing a scratch in the hardwood with my thumb. "I don't know. I think I was, at some point. Or I told myself I was. It's easy to be with someone who doesn't ask too many questions. Who doesn't hold you to anything beyond the surface."

He nodded as he listened.

"But it's lonely, too. And I don't think I realized just how much until now. I'm supposed to be working on a new book that's due in four months, and I haven't written a single word. I'm completely stuck, and the pressure's eating me alive. I don't know what to do."

He adjusted the blanket between us and leaned back on his hands. "What's it supposed to be about?"

"That's the problem," I said. "I don't know. I feel like I'm dried out. Like I've used up everything I had in me."

"Maybe you just haven't found the right story yet."

I looked at him. "You think it's that simple?"

He gave a small, crooked smile. "I never said it was simple. I just think maybe you're overthinking it."

I let out a breath. "I don't even know who I am half the time. I used to be so sure about everything. What I wanted. Who I wanted. But lately it feels like I'm just pretending I've got it all together, when really I'm still waiting for something to finally make sense."

He shifted a little closer, his voice quiet but certain. "You don't have to have it all figured out," he said. "There's no rulebook. Just take it one day at a time."

I let the words hang in the air for a second, then offered a small smile. "Okay, enough about me," I said, nudging him lightly with my knee. "Your turn in the hot seat."

He looked over at me, curious. "Oh yeah?"

I met his eyes. "Why haven't you settled down?"

He blinked like I'd caught him off guard.

"I mean," I went on quickly, "you're smart, you've got your life together, you're successful, kind. You've always been the type girls notice. So what's the deal?"

He laughed under his breath and rubbed at his jaw, like he was trying to come up with something clever. "Wow. No pressure."

"I'm just curious," I said, softer now.

He leaned back a little, looking toward the candle burning low on the coffee table. "I guess I've just...been busy," he said after a pause. "Work, deadlines, late nights. It's easy to make excuses when you've always got something occupying your time."

"For five years? Uh-uh, no way, That's not a real answer."

He glanced over at me. "No, I guess it's not."

I stayed quiet as I waited for him to continue.

"I think I just got good at being alone," he said eventually. "You do it long enough, and it stops feeling temporary. Starts to feel like maybe that's just how things are."

My chest ached in a way I didn't expect. That didn't sound anything like the Miles I once knew. "That sounds really lonely."

His mouth twitched like he wanted to argue, but he didn't. He looked at me instead and said, "Yeah. Sometimes it is."

The room felt warmer all of a sudden, but not because of the candles that surrounded us. It was because of him. Because this was a new version of Miles that didn't hide behind a joke or deflect with a smirk. The one who let me see past the surface, even if it was just for a moment.

The cold had begun to creep in around the windows and through the floorboards. I shivered, pulling the blanket a little tighter around my shoulders.

Miles stood and stretched, glancing toward the windows. "It's already dropped another ten degrees since the power went out," he said. "If it keeps falling like this, it's going to get freezing in here tonight."

I nodded slowly, tugging at the blanket. My toes were already cold through my socks.

He hesitated, rubbing the back of his neck like he was weighing something.

"Look," he started, his tone gentler now. "I know this might be weird to ask. And if you're not comfortable, that's totally fine. But I think it'd be smarter if we both slept in the bed tonight."

I glanced up, eyebrows raised.

"Just to stay warm," he added quickly. "I won't cross any lines, Keira. I won't do anything you don't want me to. You know me."

My chest tightened a little at the way he said it. Like the thought had been on his mind for a while, but he'd waited until it felt right to say it.

"I just—" He looked at me, and there was no tension in his face, only concern. "I don't want you freezing alone."

I looked down at my hands. "We used to share the bed all the time and never thought twice about it."

He smiled faintly. "Exactly."

A pause stretched between us, soft and full.

"Okay," I said finally. "Just to stay warm."

"Just to stay warm," he repeated, giving a small nod, like he was promising it to himself too.

We blew out the last of the candles in the living room, the apartment sinking into darkness as we moved quietly through it, guided only by the soft glow of our phone screens. When we reached his room, we began lighting a few more candles, their flicker casting warm shadows across the walls.

He pulled back the covers as I stood in the doorway, holding the t-shirt he'd given me.

I hesitated for a second, unsure if I should change here or sneak off to the bathroom. But the bathroom was pitch black, colder, and honestly, it felt stupid to be shy after everything.

Still, I lingered just a little too long before I said, "Mind if I just change here?"

He jumped into bed quickly. "Yeah—no, that's fine. I'll cover my eyes." He bowed his head into his hands like we were still sixteen. "Promise I won't peek."

I smiled despite myself. "Still such a gentleman."

I slipped out of my jeans, peeled off his sweater, and tugged the oversized t-shirt over my head. It was soft and worn thin in places, hanging just past mid-thigh. I breathed in the faint smell of his cologne still on the shirt; God he smelled so good. I pulled my hair up into a loose knot and tried not to think about how exposed I felt.

"Okay," I said quietly.

Miles turned around.

His eyes met mine for a moment before they flicked down, briefly on instinct, then right back up. His mouth opened like he might say something, but he didn't. He just stared at me, a small smile threatening to break onto his face.

I stood there, barefoot at the foot of his bed in nothing but his shirt, and for a second neither of us moved.

"I have to say, it looks way better on you," he said finally as he brought his arms around his knees and leaned forward, his voice low.

I laughed once, a little breathless. "Why, thank you."

I climbed into bed next to him and pulled the blankets over myself. Our backs to the edges, our faces turned toward each other. Not touching, not even close, but the space between us felt small in a way that made me ache.

"You warm enough?" he asked.

I nodded. "Yeah. I'm okay."

I tucked the blankets tighter around myself and watched the way his profile caught the faint moonlight from the window. It reminded me of those nights when we were teenagers, when I'd sneak into his room after our parents fell asleep, slipping beneath his covers without saying a word.

He never made it a big deal. I just needed to be near someone, and he always let me stay. Sometimes we'd whisper about nothing in particular until I fell asleep with my head on his shoulder. It had been years, but this felt achingly familiar.

"Remember when I used to call you late at night?" I asked, breaking the silence. "You'd tell me stories until I could fall asleep."

Miles smiled in the dark. "Of course I remember. It was usually on school nights, and your mom would get so pissed if she caught you. I remember one about a princess who—"

"That was my favorite!" I said, beating him to it.

"You fell asleep halfway through it every time."

"I liked the sound of your voice," I said softly. "I think that's what made it easy to sleep."

He didn't answer for a moment. When he did, his voice was gentler than before. "Want me to tell you one now?"

I smiled. "Yeah. I'd like that."

So he did.

My eyes drifted shut somewhere in the middle. The cold was still there, but it didn't seem to matter anymore.

Not with him beside me.

Not with the sound of his voice pulling me under, safe and warm.

***

THEN — AGE 15

PORTLAND, MAINE

I wasn't supposed to be up.

The house was dark, and I could hear the hum of the dishwasher down the hall and my parents' TV faintly through the wall. But I was under the covers, curled on my side with the bulky cordless landline phone pressed to my chest, knowing my mom would lose it if she knew I had the phone this late on a school night.

I had pulled the blanket over my head to block out as much sound as I could, heart pounding even though I wasn't doing anything that bad. Just maybe a little against the rules.

I pressed speed dial 3.

He picked up on the second ring.

"Hello?" Miles's voice sounded sleepy, and I immediately felt a little guilty.

"It's me," I whispered, trying not to sound too loud. "Did I wake you up?"

He yawned. "Kind of. But it's okay. You alright?"

I nodded even though he couldn't see me. "I can't sleep."

There was a pause, just long enough that I almost regretted calling.

Then he softly asked, "Do you want me to tell you a story?"

A smile tugged at my lips. "Yeah."

He always did this for me when I couldn't fall asleep. He'd make something up on the spot, always ridiculous and sweet. Sometimes it was about aliens disguised as humans, trying to blend in by working at a diner in New Jersey. Or a ghost who was afraid of haunted houses. But tonight, he started off differently.

"Okay. Once upon a time," he said, "there was a princess. She wasn't a regular princess. She didn't live in a castle, and she didn't wear crowns made from jewels. But she was still the most beautiful girl in her kingdom."

I blushed in the dark, cheeks warm under the blanket. "Oh yeah?" I asked, teasing a little.

"Yeah," he said seriously. "She had this laugh that made everyone around her feel better. And she was brave. She stood up to the king once when he tried to outlaw candy."

I giggled. "That's very specific."

"Really, it happened," he said. "I'm just the narrator."

I let him keep going, his voice a little raspy with sleep. In the story, the princess loved to wander the woods and name all the trees. One day, she found a boy hiding in one of them, lost and covered in paint from a failed attempt at making his own map to find his way home. They became friends. He made her laugh, and she made him feel like he wasn't invisible. And then she invited him to live in her kingdom.

I didn't ask who he meant.

I didn't need to.

At some point, my hand slid under my cheek, and I just listened. Everything started to drift off. My room, the rules, the weight of being fifteen and not knowing what to do with the way my heart picked up when he said my name. He didn't know it, but I sometimes called just to hear his voice, not because I couldn't sleep.

I think we both knew there was something different between us. We just hadn't figured out how to talk about it yet. Or maybe we weren't ready.

He was still talking softly, about the girl and the boy building a treehouse in the woods, when my eyes started to fall shut.

"Miles?" I whispered

"Yeah?"

"Thanks."

He was quiet for a second.

"Always."

The story drifted off. And not long after that, so did we. On the phone, still connected. I remember hearing his breathing settle, and that was the last thing I held onto before I fell asleep.

Chapter 17

KEIRA

PRESENT DAY

CHICAGO, ILLINOIS

I woke up warm. Warmer than I'd felt in days. It took a second for my brain to catch up with my body, still heavy with sleep, but the realization came gently.

Miles.

His arm was around my waist, our legs tangled loosely beneath the blanket. He was behind me, his breath steady against the back of my neck.

I didn't panic. I didn't stiffen or pull away. I just lay there quietly next to him, imagining another life where this was my every day.

We must've shifted in the night, unconsciously pulling close as the temperature dropped. The power hadn't come back on. The room was quiet, still dark but glowing faintly from the edges of the curtains.

Carefully, I slipped out from under the covers without waking him. I stood there for a second, watching the way he stayed curled on his side, his hair rumpled, his face relaxed in a way I hadn't seen since we were kids. I wanted to reach out to him. I so badly just wanted to slip my arm around him and curl up close.

Instead, I padded softly down the hallway and shut the bathroom door behind me.

Steam curled through the bathroom as I turned on the water. With the power still out, I knew the hot water wouldn't last long, so I needed to take advantage of it while I could.

I tugged off his shirt slowly and stepped into the shower. The heat wrapped around me, loosening the tension I hadn't known I was holding in my shoulders, my chest, my jaw.

Leaning my forehead against the tile, I let out a slow breath.

I shouldn't have liked waking up like that as much as I did. I know it wasn't right. But how was I supposed to fight a complicated history?

It was easier to act like life was simple. To ignore the ring sitting tucked in the back of my dresser at home and the man who had stayed faithfully beside me for three years, even though none of this was fair to him.

I'd have to talk to Dylan soon. I knew I owed him an explanation, for the way I'd been acting since I landed in Chicago. Hell, for the way I'd been acting even before that.

I couldn't help but wonder how I would feel if the situation were reversed? If Dylan were pulling away, leaving on a trip without his engagement ring, staying in the apartment of a woman he'd never mentioned before. I wouldn't like it. I wouldn't trust it. And if that would hurt me, then I had to face what my choices were doing to him.

I ran my hands through my hair and let the water soak in, wishing it could rinse the guilt out of me just as easily. Even though nothing physical had happened between Miles and me, there was a dull, persistent weight in my chest, like I'd crossed some invisible line anyway. I'd never woken up next to Dylan and felt what I felt this morning. I'd never looked at him and had to fight the urge to memorize every inch of his face while he slept. But I also never wondered why that was. I never questioned any of the things that made me unsure about Dylan.

There was something about Miles that still got to me. Not because he was some fantasy from my past, but because, somehow, he still felt like the most real thing in the room. Being around him stirred things up I thought I'd buried. Not just memories, but possibilities.

I shut off the water and stepped out, wrapping myself in one of Miles's thick towels. The bathroom was fogged over, the mirror completely steamed.

I wiped a corner with my hand and caught my reflection. My cheeks were rosier, hair damp, and my eyes heavy with too much emotion. I took a deep breath and held it, trying to give my head a moment of clarity.

I got dressed in a clean baggy sweater and sweatpants that I snuck from Miles' wardrobe this morning. It was still cold in the apartment, though the snow had finally stopped. The windows were coated with frost, and the sun tried to peek out between the clouds. I stood there for a moment, admiring the beauty of the stillness.

I padded barefoot into the kitchen, wondering if Miles was awake yet.

He was.

He stood at the stove in his sweats and a t-shirt, barefoot and half asleep, stirring something in a pot that smelled faintly like oatmeal. His hair was sticking up at odd angles, and when he turned and saw me, he smiled like it was the most natural thing in the world.

"Morning," he said, voice scratchy.

"Hey," I said, my tone soft. "You're making breakfast? How did you manage to get the stove to work?"

"The old-fashioned way, by striking a match. Luckily the gas still works. And besides, you did dinner last night. I figured we were taking turns," he said, turning back to the stove.

"My hero," I said with a smile.

"Bad news, I don't trust the food in the fridge, but the good news is we've got instant oatmeal, so we won't have to starve."

"Good enough for me," I said. The way he said our food made my stomach flutter.

I moved quietly across the kitchen, suddenly hyper-aware of every sound. The quiet clink of the spoon. The creak of the floor beneath my feet.

"Sleep okay?" he asked after a moment.

"Yeah. I really did."

He glanced over his shoulder at me. His smile was subtle but warm.

"Me too."

I sat down at the counter and pulled my sleeves over my hands, watching him move around the kitchen like it was second nature.

He glanced at the clock and then back at me. "Hey, I meant to tell you, I have to head into the office for a bit. It'll probably take me a couple of hours."

I blinked. "You're working today?"

"No, not at all, but I've got a few files I need to grab," he said, wiping his hands on a dish towel. "A deadline moved up on a client project, and I just got the text this morning. Naturally, everything important is still sitting on my desk, because why wouldn't it be?" He pulled out something small and shiny from his pocket. "I've got a key, though, so I won't have to bother anyone. I'll be quick."

"You sure it's safe to go out?" I asked, glancing toward the window.

The snow had stopped, but the streets were still somewhat buried, sidewalks were barely visible beneath thick drifts of white.

He nodded. "Yeah. I'll stick to the main roads. Should be manageable. The plows have been going to town the last few days."

I didn't doubt that. Miles had always been the type to quietly take care of things without making a big deal out of it. Still, something about the idea of him out there alone made me nervous, and I didn't know how to say that without it sounding more than I meant.

"Well, be careful," I said instead.

"Don't you worry about me, Sullivan. I've got plenty of dry goods in the pantry if you get hungry and books on the shelf for your reading pleasure,"

He gave me a small smile, the kind that felt more like a reassurance than a goodbye.

"Thanks, I'm sure I'll be fine. I'll just grab your copy of *Pride and Prejudice* and read it again for the thousandth time."

He let out a laugh and grabbed his coat from the hook by the door and tugged on a beanie, then glanced over his shoulder one last time before heading out. "Call me if you need me."

The door clicked softly shut behind him, and the apartment felt instantly quieter. I stood there for a second, listening to the silence settle in.

It was strange, being here without him.

Not just in his space, but in this moment that had been so much about us these past few days.

I decided that I wasn't ready to sit with those thoughts just yet.

So I took my time cleaning up the dishes from breakfast. I rinsed the mugs, wiped down the stove, and folded the dish towel back over the handle the way he had. It felt nice.

Grounding. Like something I could've done a hundred times before.

The sun was brighter today, casting a muted light across the floorboards as I walked through the living room. I browsed Miles' collection of novels that were on his bookshelf and picked one up, curling into the corner chair near the window. I adored that he had a copy of Pride and Prejudice.

Everyone focused on the romance between Darcy and Elizabeth, but I'd always been drawn to Jane and Mr. Bingley. Two friends circling something deeper, both too unsure to say it out loud. There was something tender in that hesitation, in the way they kept hoping the other felt the same. Maybe because it reminded me of what I'd never quite dared to face in my own life.

I read a few chapters, sipping hot tea I made with one of the bags I found in the cupboard, which thankfully had been chamomile, and let the warmth settle into me. There was something quietly surreal about how at ease I felt.

The hours slipped by without urgency, and for the first time in a long while, I wasn't thinking about what came next. Inside these walls, it felt like I'd stepped back into some place safe.

At some point, I got up and turned on the wireless Bluetooth speaker sitting on the shelf. I was so thankful that it was already charged from the night before. I picked a playlist at random and let it hum quietly through the space. I made the bed. Folded the blankets in the living room. I even cleaned the bathroom mirror, wiping away the streaks from the steam this morning. It was borderline embarrassing how much I enjoyed it.

By noon, I was getting hungry again. I found a can of lentil soup in the cabinet and warmed it on the stove while watching a pair of birds hop along the fire escape outside.

After lunch, I wandered the apartment again, tracing my hand along the spines of Miles's books and photos on the shelves, glancing at the old record player tucked beside the bookshelf.

I flipped through his records, fingers brushing past an old 80s movie soundtrack and a worn Snow Patrol album, when something caught my eye. A thin paper bag was wedged between them and had been barely noticeable. I pulled it out and peeked inside. My breath caught suddenly. *Parachutes.*

I couldn't believe he had it. The album we used to play on repeat late at night, talking about everything and nothing. The album that had our song on it. But it was still in the bag, untouched. That part made my chest ache a little. I started to wonder what other pieces of us still lived in this apartment. And that's when I remembered the box.

I didn't hesitate this time. I probably should've, but I didn't. He hadn't hidden it, and he'd told me to make myself at home. So I did.

I walked into the bedroom under the pretense of tidying up some more, but the excuse was flimsy at best. I folded the throw at the end of the bed, straightened out the books on the side table, and ran my fingers along the windowsill just to keep my hands busy. But really, I was stalling.

The moment I opened the closet, my eyes went straight to it. Plain. Old. My name is written across the side in Miles's writing. Like it had been waiting for me.

I stood there for a moment, staring up at it.

And then I reached for it.

No more excuses. No more pretending I was doing anything else.

I pulled the box down slowly and carried it to the bed, setting it in my lap.

My fingers hovered over the edge.

And then I opened it.

Inside, it wasn't chaos. It wasn't dusty or neglected. Everything was neat. Purposeful. Like he had opened this box more than once over the years.

The first thing I saw was a folded piece of lined notebook paper.

The corner was torn, the ink smudged in places. I opened it slowly, already recognizing the silly doodle of a stick figure holding up a sign that said Save me from algebra. My handwriting. I remembered the day. I'd drawn it during sophomore year and passed it to him under the desk during Mr. Green's endless lecture. Miles had stifled a laugh, and then sketched a second figure hanging from a graph line. It had seemed so dumb at the time.

Just something to get through the hour. But here it was.

I laughed quietly, my eyes stinging. That paper wasn't just a memory; it was proof of a hundred moments like that. Private little worlds we used to build out of boredom and proximity. I'd forgotten what it was like to be known in that easy, casual way.

I reached in again and pulled out a strip of photo booth pictures. My breath caught. I hadn't seen these in years.

The two of us at a street fair; me with a funnel cake in one hand, him wearing those stupid glow-in-the-dark glasses we won at a dart game. The first frame was blurry. The second showed me laughing so hard my eyes were nearly shut. The third was Miles pretending to kiss my cheek while I dramatically recoiled.

I traced the outline of his face with my thumb. We were so close to something back then.

Always on the edge of it.

The Donald Duck keychain was next. Its colors were faded, and the paint chipped at the edges, but it was unmistakable. I brought it back for him after my trip to Disney World when we were fifteen. My mom got so irritated with me on that trip because I was constantly on the phone with him in our hotel room.

It was a silly, last-minute gift I picked up at the airport gift shop. He used to have it clipped to his favorite backpack. I remembered standing in the store, unsure of what to get him, and grabbing the keychain because Donald had always reminded me of Miles somehow. Grumpy, loyal, low-key hilarious when he wanted to be. I turned the keychain over in my hand, smiling despite the lump in my throat.

Then I pulled out the friendship bracelet. Blue and green thread, knotted unevenly in places. My fingers ran over it slowly. We must've made those when we were thirteen, sitting on the steps outside the craft cabin. I made one for him, and he made one for me. I lost mine in the lake during our second year of camp. But he...he had kept his. All this time.

And finally, at the very bottom, I found something I hadn't expected at all.

My stuffed animal, but not just any stuffed animal—my brown koala bear, the one I'd had since I was five. The one that sang when you pushed its tummy. I must have left it during the last time I crashed at his place before he left. I thought I'd misplaced it or accidentally left it behind somewhere. I couldn't believe he'd found it... and kept it. All this time. My breath caught in my throat as I lifted it out, the fabric worn smooth with age and love.

He kept the things from our past that were important to him. Everything that made us...us. The things no one else would understand. It was proof. Proof that he had loved me. And that's when I realized: he never left me, he took all of me with him.

And now, five years later, sitting here in his room with a box of our memories in my lap, I knew that I'd never stopped carrying him either. I'd just buried him in a small box of my own, tucked away deep inside of me.

I started gently placing everything back, folding the note and lining up the photo strip as neatly as I could. But my hands shook. I picked up the open box and held it there, unmoving, staring down at my name.

I was still sitting on the edge of the bed when I heard the front door open and shut, unaware of how much time had gone by. I didn't move. I couldn't. My hands were now resting in my lap, fingers lightly brushing the frayed edge of the friendship bracelet he'd never thrown away.

The box sat open beside me like some cruel time capsule, every item inside spilling over with meaning I couldn't un-feel now that I knew.

I could hear him taking off his boots, the familiar rhythm of his steps down the hall, and then his pause at the door. He must've seen me then. Two tears had fallen without my permission, and I hadn't even wiped them away.

"Keira?" he said, his voice careful. Like he already knew

something was coming. His gaze dropped to my hands. "Where…did you find that?"

I didn't answer. I couldn't even look at him yet. I kept my eyes down on the keychain in the hand opposite the bracelet, turning it slowly in my palm. The tiny, scuffed figure of Donald Duck stared back at me.

Miles stepped in, slower this time. I could feel him hovering near the doorway, unsure of what he was walking into.

Then I looked up, and the wall finally broke. "Why did you let me go?"

He didn't respond at first. Maybe he thought we could just keep pretending that what happened between us five years ago was just a mistake and that we could easily start over.

But I was tired. Tired of pretending it hadn't mattered. Tired of acting like I wasn't still carrying the weight of his silence from all those years ago. Tired of pretending that I hadn't spent my entire life in love with him.

The adrenaline hit my bloodstream, and I stood up, not even trying to hide the tears that kept coming. "I waited for you to call," I said. "I waited every single day for weeks. I made excuses for you. Told myself you were just settling in, or you'd lost your charger, or maybe something happened to your phone. I let myself believe you were coming back for me!"

He looked like he'd been punched directly in the gut. "Keira—"

"No, Miles," I cut in, softer now, but not backing down. "You let me go. And I had to carry that and act like it didn't wreck me."

He stepped forward like he wanted to close the space between us, but he didn't. His jaw was tight. His hands were in fists at his sides, like he didn't trust them not to reach for me.

"I thought I was doing the right thing," he said quietly. "I thought if I stayed away, you'd be able to move on. You had so much ahead of you, Keira. We never knew what we were. It was never the right time."

"That wasn't your decision to make!" I said. "You don't get to decide that for me and disappear like I was just something you were finished with before we even started."

The silence between us was suddenly louder than anything else.

I looked back at the box. At the pieces of us that he kept hidden, tucked away in his closet like a secret he couldn't bear to throw out.

"So what the hell is this, then?" I asked, nodding toward it. "What does all that mean to you? That you literally have me here tucked away in your closet. In your go damn closet, Miles."

He didn't answer.

Then I finally said it. After seventeen years, one of us had to. "I loved you. God, I loved you so much I didn't know what to do with it. You were in everything: my thoughts, my writing, my dreams. And even after you left, even after the silence, I still held on to you. Like some part of me believed that if I held on tight enough, you'd feel it from wherever you were."

I took a breath. My voice was shaking but steady, like my heart had finally chosen to speak after all this time. "You were the first person who ever saw me. Not just the version of me that smiled and made jokes and kept it all together. You saw the girl behind that. The one who doubted herself. Who had trouble sleeping most nights and got scared of thunderstorms and didn't always know how to ask for help when she needed it."

My eyes burned, but I didn't look away.

"You say you left because you thought it was better for me. That you didn't want to hold me back. But all that did was leave me wondering what I did wrong. Why I wasn't enough for you to stay. I'm tired of pretending I'm over it. I'm tired of swallowing down everything I should've said years ago. I love you, Miles. I never stopped. And I don't know what that means now, or what I'm supposed to do about it, or what it says about me that I'm still standing here after everything…but I do. I love you. And no matter where we are, how much time has gone by, or who we're with, part of me always will."

There was a silence between us so thick I could feel it pressing against my chest. All the unsaid things, all the time that passed without explanation, it was unbearable. But then he looked at me. And I saw it there. Everything he'd been holding back.

He crossed the last bit of space between us and knelt in front of me, gently taking my face in his hands like he was afraid I might break.

"I didn't stop loving you," he whispered, voice raw. "Not for a second. And when I left, I thought it was the right thing. But shit, Keira, I haven't felt right since."

My breath caught. I stared at him, wide-eyed, as his thumbs brushed away the tears that were falling steadily now.

"I know I hurt you when I left," he said quietly. "But we're older now, Keira. Of all the things I've done wrong, all the choices I wish I could take back, losing you is the one that still keeps me up at night. And I refuse to make the same mistake twice."

His eyes flicked down to my lips, just for a second, then back.

"If I kiss you right now, I won't be able to stop," he said.

"Then don't," I whispered.

That was all it took.

He leaned in and kissed me like he'd been waiting five years just to feel my mouth against his again. His hands stayed on my face, grounding me as my fingers curled into his shirt. The kiss deepened, pulled from something that was living inside of us, something that was still ours.

We weren't the same kids anymore. We were older, trying to navigate through life without each other, and carrying more weight than we knew what to do with. But in that moment, none of it mattered. Not the time we lost. Not the man waiting for me at home. Not the storm outside. Just him. Just me. Just this.

And finally, finally, the space between us was gone.

Chapter 18

PRESENT DAY

CHICAGO, ILLINOIS

I didn't know where to touch her first.

I just knew I couldn't stop.

Her mouth crashed into mine, her hands everywhere, and I couldn't breathe without needing more of her. Everything in me was lit up and trembling and aching all at once.

I backed her up until her spine met the wall. Her lips parted in a gasp, but she didn't stop me. Instead, she pulled me closer, tighter. I lifted her without thinking, hands gripping the backs of her thighs, as she wrapped her legs around me, claiming me like I belonged to her.

Like she was afraid I'd disappear again.

Her arms looped around my neck, and I held her there against the wall, heart pounding so hard I could feel it everywhere. Her forehead met mine, both of us breathing heavy, every inch of her pressed against me.

"Tell me you want this," I said, voice rough, barely holding it together.

"I've always wanted this," she whispered, eyes locked on mine. "I want you."

That was all I needed to hear.

I kissed her again, hard and desperate. Needing to taste every inch of her and make up for lost time. Her fingers tangled in my hair as I rocked against her, hips chasing friction like she couldn't help it. Her breath hitched when I pressed closer, and I felt her coming apart in my arms.

She was warm and soft and wild against me, and I didn't care about anything else. The past. The pain. The five years of silence. It all fell away the moment she moaned my name.

I carried her to the bed and laid her down gently. She looked up at me with wide, unguarded eyes, her chest rising and falling, silently begging me not to stop. So I didn't.

I ran my hand down her side, slow and deliberate, feeling the way her body leaned into mine, craving more. I kissed her collarbone, her shoulder, the curve of her neck. Every inch I could reach, I claimed, until she arched into me like it physically hurt to be apart.

The rest of our clothes came off in quiet, breathless pieces, the air between us thick with need. I took my time, letting my hands learn her again. And when I finally slid into her, she let out a quiet, broken sound that had been part relief and part need.

There was no fear. No hesitation. Just us.

She took my face in her hands and held me there. I kissed her through every slow thrust, every breathless moan, every whisper of my name that slipped past her lips.

Her legs wrapped around my waist, pulling me closer, deeper, like she couldn't get enough. I moved slowly, letting her feel all of me, as she buried her face in my neck, breathing hard, her body trembling slightly beneath mine. Every shift of her hips, every quiet moan against my skin, felt like a plea for more.

And I gave it to her, again and again, until we both finally came undone.

***

We stayed close, arms and legs intertwined, holding on like the moment might slip away if we moved too fast. Her forehead rested against mine, skin damp, cheeks flushed, her body still trembling faintly from everything we'd just done. I didn't let her go. I couldn't. My hands stayed on her back, fingers tracing the curve of her spine, trying to memorize the shape of her body.

I'd never felt anything like that in my life.

We'd had sex before. More than once, more than a few times, actually. It wasn't like this was new. I knew her body. Knew the way her breath caught when I touched the inside of her thigh, the soft sound she made when I kissed just below her ear. It had always been something we fell into without thinking.

But this time was different.

There was a slowness to it. Like we were both aware of what it meant to be here now, after everything. I'd touched her differently. Not like I was trying to control something, but like I was trying to learn her all over again. And maybe, in a way, I was.

Her fingers curled against my back, not out of habit but intention. Her eyes didn't look through me. They held me. And something in my chest tightened in a way that had nothing to do with lust.

I still didn't know what we were. I didn't know where any of this was going. But in that moment, with her next to me, breath warm against my neck, I knew one thing with complete clarity: I couldn't let her slip away again.

She was quiet, eyes half closed, her hand resting gently against my chest as my heartbeat finally started to slow. She looked different now. Beautiful in a way that hit me deep.

I pressed a kiss to her forehead, then one to her shoulder. She didn't pull away. Her fingers curled into the sheets, and when I moved to lie beside her, she followed without hesitation, pulling the blanket over both of us as she nestled into my side.

She didn't say a word. She just exhaled, slow and deep, her hand sliding across my chest, tracing shapes with her fingers.

I thought maybe she'd started to fall asleep.

But then, her voice cut through the dark. "What are we doing, Miles?"

She didn't look at me when she said it. She kept her head tucked against my shoulder, her hand now resting over my heart.

I didn't answer right away. Because I didn't know. Because I didn't want to ruin it. Because everything still felt fragile.

But lying to her now would've been worse than silence.

"I don't know," I said softly. "But I do know I want more." I pressed my lips to her forehead and spoke. "I want this. I want you. Every day for the rest of my life."

She was quiet again. A beat. Two. Then she pulled back enough to look at me.

"You seriously mean that? You actually want to do this for real this time?" she said, her voice barely more than a pleading whisper.

I felt the breath go out of me. I leaned in, pressing my forehead to hers. Our noses brushed.

Our lips hovered, close enough to feel the tremble between us.

"I love you, Keira," I said quietly. "I mean every word."

She kissed me, soft at first, like she needed to feel the words on my mouth, like she didn't trust them until she tasted them. But then it deepened. Her hands slid into my hair again.

Mine gripped her hips, and the space between us disappeared all over again.

I felt the press of her body against mine as she shifted back over me, straddling my waist. Her fingers splayed against my chest. My hands were locked on her thighs. Her eyes caught mine as she guided us back to each other.

She rocked her hips against mine and leaned in close, her lips brushing the edge of my ear. "I love you too."

And I answered her with the only thing I had left. My hands, my mouth, my body.

Everything I had.

All of it hers.

***

THEN — AGE 21

LOON MOUNTAIN

LINCOLN, NEW HAMPSHIRE

I was half convinced I'd broken something.

Keira laughed the whole way down the last ski run, practically gliding, while I fell for the third time in five minutes. I was sore, freezing, and starving, but I'd never been happier.

We'd been on the mountain all day, chasing fresh powder and each other, stopping only long enough to gulp water or shake snow out of our jackets. The sun had started to dip behind the ridge, casting everything in that soft, golden haze, and she looked back at me just before we reached the bottom, cheeks flushed, hair peeking out of her helmet, eyes bright.

"You alive?" she called out, breathless, grinning.

"Barely." I groaned, dragging myself upright.

We unstrapped our boards and trudged to the lodge, boots clomping against the wooden stairs. Keira pushed open the door to the restaurant with her hip and led the way to a booth in the back, already tugging off her gloves.

She peeled off her jacket, tossed her helmet beside her, and leaned back in the booth with a satisfied sigh. "That was amazing. You wiped out like, six times."

"Three," I corrected, sliding in across from her. "And at least two were graceful."

"You flailed around like a fish out of water, Miles. I thought you were gonna take out that whole group lesson at one point."

I cracked a smile, shaking out my damp hair. "I was going for style points."

We ordered without even glancing at the menu—Caesar salad and buffalo chicken tenders, our usual lazy go-tos when we were at the lodge.

Our boots clunked together under the table as we stretched out, muscles aching in that satisfying way. Keira reached across the table and stole my water without asking, chugging half of it before setting it down with a dramatic gasp.

"I feel reborn," she said.

"You sure as hell don't look it," I said.

She flipped me off, then gave me a soft and radiant smile, like it was meant just for me.

When the food came, it was almost offensive how good it was. The salad was ice cold, the dressing tangy, croutons perfectly crunchy. The tenders were hot and crispy and drenched in sauce. Keira dunked hers in blue cheese, made a low, ridiculous moan, and closed her eyes.

"If heaven exists," she murmured, "it tastes exactly like this."

I cocked an eyebrow. "That better not be the best moan I hear from you this weekend."

She snorted. "Relax. You've gotten some pretty decent ones out of me over the years."

"Decent?" I gave her a look.

"Fine. Good," she allowed. "Like a solid eight out of ten."

"Eight?" I dragged my hand down my face. "Wow. I've been living a lie."

Keira laughed so hard she accidentally choked on a piece of lettuce and had to sip her water again while I tried to hold back a grin.

The couple at the table next to us moved to a different one, clearly annoyed by the noise. We didn't care. I was staring at her, flushed and glowing and alive in a way I'd only ever seen on days like this. She was wild, free, and just a little over the top in the best way.

She caught me looking and smirked.

"What?" she said, wiping sauce from the corner of her mouth.

"Nothing," I said, because if I said what I was really thinking, she probably would've thrown something at me for being so corny.

When we got back to the room, our limbs were tired, our bodies aching, skin still stinging from the cold. Keira grabbed her bag and disappeared into the bathroom. I heard the shower turn on, the curtain rustle, the hum of her voice starting and stopping in broken little bursts of whatever song she was trying to sing.

I loved the sound of her voice. She had this quiet, effortless talent. She was an incredible singer who'd never admit it, not to anyone. She played guitar just as beautifully, but she always brushed it off, calling herself a campfire musician, like that was all she ever wanted to be.

I lay back on the bed, arms behind my head, staring at the ceiling and trying not to think about the fact that she was naked just a few feet away.

Ten minutes later, the door creaked open, and she stepped out barefoot, wrapped in one of my t-shirts, hair damp and hanging in soft waves over her shoulders. Her legs were bare, her skin flushed pink from the hot water. She looked clean and warm and a little sleepy.

"What?" she asked, giving me a look.

"Nothing," I said again, trying not to smile. "Just...wasn't expecting you to look that good tonight."

She rolled her eyes and crossed the room, sliding open the glass door to the patio. Cold air rushed in immediately, but she didn't flinch. She always loved to have the windows open, even on cold nights.

She stepped outside and leaned her arms on the railing, staring out into the black silhouette of the mountains. The snow fell, soft and silent.

K.L. Sawyer

I got up and followed, stepping behind her and wrapping my arms around her waist. She leaned back into me without a word.

"I'll never get tired of this view," she whispered.

I looked down at her then, knowing exactly how she felt. "Me either," I said, kissing her shoulder.

She turned in my arms to face me. That's when I kissed her, deep and slow. Everything in me tightened at the way she melted into me. Her hands found the back of my neck, pulling me closer. I could taste the warmth of the hot chocolate she had still on her lips, and could feel the heat rising despite the cold air around us.

She took my hands and led me back inside, never breaking our kiss.

***

NOW

The morning light had just started to break through the curtains. I lay there, feeling the warmth of her body press against mine. Her leg was thrown over my thigh, her hand resting on my chest, fingers twitching slightly in her sleep.

She looked peaceful. Tired, but refreshed. Her lips were parted, her hair tangled against the pillow, the edge of the blanket pulled up just beneath her shoulder.

I couldn't remember the last time I'd woken up comfortable and genuinely happy. It should've felt unfamiliar, but it didn't. It felt like something I'd been missing for years.

I traced my thumb slowly along the curve of her spine, careful not to wake her. I didn't want to break the moment. Didn't want to think about what would happen when she opened her eyes and remembered we didn't belong to each other.

The night before lingered on my skin. The way she touched me. The way she said my name.

The way we made each other come undone so easily.

I'd spent five years trying to forget what it felt like to be loved by her.

Last night made me realize I never really had.

She stirred a little, her leg shifting, her fingers tightening over my chest, and for a moment, I wondered what she was dreaming about. Her face scrunched for half a second, then softened again.

I could've stayed like that all morning.

Eventually, she blinked, slow and hazy. Her lashes fluttered, and her gaze moved up toward me. Her expression didn't change, not at first. She just looked at me like she was still figuring out whether this was real.

"Hi," she whispered.

I smiled. "Hey."

She didn't move. Just lay there, her hand still on my chest, then she gave a deep sigh. "You're warm."

I let out a soft breath and buried my face in her neck. "You steal all the covers."

"Some things never change, right?" she said

I brushed her hair away from her face, letting my fingers rest just behind her ear for a moment. "You okay?"

She nodded. But it was the kind of nod that wasn't a yes or a no, but instead a way to move past the question.

I didn't push her to talk. There was no reason to. Everything that needed to be said had already passed between us in the dark. I leaned in and kissed her gently. She kissed me back with the same softness, her hand sliding up the side of my neck, her lips warm and unhurried.

We didn't say a word. We just held there for a moment, forehead to forehead, the air still and calm around us.

Eventually, we got out of bed. She stood and stretched, tugging one of my shirts from the floor and slipping it on. I watched her move through the room, barefoot, hair a little tangled, face still quiet from sleep. She looked at home in my space, like nothing between us had ever broken.

I started the coffee while she sat on the edge of the counter with her knees pulled up, watching me move around the kitchen. She reached for my mug without asking, took a sip, wrinkled her nose a little at the bitterness, then took another anyway.

"I can't believe you still drink it black," she said, a small smile tugging at the corner of her mouth.

"And you're still pretending to like it."

She gave a soft laugh and shook her head. "It's not that bad. Just...intense."

"Like me?"

She raised an eyebrow. "You think you're intense?"

I shrugged. "Hey, I'm intense in all the best ways."

She took another sip, grimacing slightly. "Still bitter."

"The coffee?"

She gave me a look. "You."

That made me smile. Even I had to admit, I loved the way she teased me.

The fridge was still dead, so breakfast was basic. I grabbed the oats from the cabinet while she turned on the kettle and pulled out her favorite tea from the cupboard. I queued up some music on my phone, something low and relaxed, just enough to keep the quiet from feeling too heavy.

The way we moved around each other felt familiar, easy, like muscle memory. She handed me the cinnamon without me having to ask. I stirred the pot while she leaned back against the counter and waited. It was simple, but it felt good.

We ate breakfast, and after we cleaned up, she drifted into the living room and pulled the old navy blue blanket from behind the couch. I followed a moment later and sat down beside her, pulling her legs into my lap without asking.

She didn't resist. Just shifted a little so she could rest more comfortably against the arm of the couch. Her feet were cold, but she didn't seem to mind. I placed my hand gently on her shin, my thumb moving back and forth in a slow rhythm, and she let out a quiet breath, eyes closing as her body relaxed again.

I reached for the battered paperback on the shelf—*A Farewell to Arms*—and she gave me a look.

"Still your favorite?" she asked.

I nodded. "It's held up."

She leaned her head against the cushions and got more comfortable. "Read it to me."

So I opened the book and did just that.

The words came easily from the old, familiar phrases I'd read a hundred times before. But this time, they felt different with her beside me. More personal somehow. Like every line meant something more now than it ever had.

I kept reading, even when my voice got quieter, even when the words started to blur a little because my head was somewhere else. Somewhere just past the page. Somewhere in the space between her body and mine.

When I stopped, she didn't speak. Just lay there quietly, her breathing slow and even. We sat in that silence for a long time. And I didn't need her to fill it.

I already knew what she was thinking, because I was thinking it too.

What happens now?

Where the hell do we go from here?

Chapter 19

KIERA

PRESENT DAY

CHICAGO, ILLINOIS

The power finally came back on that morning. Businesses started opening back up, and we decided to take a walk through the snowy streets, stopping at a bakery on the corner to split a croissant. He let me have the bigger half, just like he used to. Later, we hit the grocery store and wandered into a record shop to warm up. He browsed while I stood nearby.

There were moments where our hands would find each other without thinking. Where our eyes would meet and hold for a second too long. The events that led us here may not have been perfect, but this felt like something real, something we hadn't let ourselves believe could still exist between us.

By the time the sun started to dip behind the buildings, we were back at the apartment. We moved around each other with a quiet kind of ease. Miles made dinner, and I set the table for the two of us. It felt normal. Comfortable. Like a life we could've had if things had gone differently.

We sat on the couch together after we ate, our legs tucked under blankets, a movie playing low in the background. I leaned into him without thinking, my head resting against his shoulder. He just sat there with me, like it was the most natural thing in the world.

Then my phone lit up on the coffee table.

The first time, I ignored it. Just a few buzzes, then silence. The second time, I glanced at the screen and looked away. The third time, I couldn't pretend anymore.

Miles felt me tense and looked down just as the name appeared again. Dylan.

I reached for the phone, heart pounding harder than I wanted to admit. "I should...I need to take this."

He gave a small nod, but his eyes didn't follow me as I stood up and walked into the hallway.

I closed the door to the guest room gently behind me. I sat on the edge of the bed, gripping the phone tightly in one hand while pulling a blanket over my shoulders with the other.

The phone rang until I had yet another missed call from Dylan. I decided to open my texts fully before calling him back and found the most recent one from Jess. It had been sent about an hour earlier.

> Jess: Call me when you're able. Just got off with the airline. Good news!

I didn't feel ready to talk, but I tapped her name anyway and brought the phone to my ear.

She answered on the second ring. "Keira! There you are. I've been chasing you all day."

"Yeah, I'm sorry," I said. My voice sounded thin. "It's been a bit of a day."

"I know, and you still need to fill me in. I know things have been up in the air, but we finally got word back. Your flight's booked for tomorrow evening. Chicago to Boston. Direct. You should be home before midnight."

My stomach turned. Home. The word didn't sit right. Not now. Not when I wasn't sure where that even was anymore.

"Tomorrow? Like, twenty-four hours from now?"

"Yes!" she said

"Oh…that's great," I said quietly.

"And the tour has been officially postponed. Maya made the call this afternoon. We're looking at a relaunch next summer. Fresh push. Bigger rollout. And hopefully just in time for the release of your third book. It's all probably for the best, honestly."

I nodded, even though she couldn't see me. "Right. That makes sense."

"Are you alright?" she asked after a beat. "You sound…I don't know. Off."

"I'm fine," I lied. "You know me, just a textbook overthinker. It's been a long couple of days."

"Well, try to get some rest. Once you're back, we'll regroup and set up the new calendar over brunch."

"Okay," I said. "Thanks, Jess."

She signed off cheerfully. I hung up slowly, setting the phone back down beside me, and let the silence fall again.

Tomorrow.

I was leaving tomorrow night.

I pressed my hands to my face and closed my eyes. Everything inside me felt like it was starting to collapse in on itself. I wasn't ready to leave. I wasn't ready to walk out of this space, this feeling, this glimpse of something I hadn't realized I still needed until I found myself inside it again.

Being with Miles this week had all felt so normal. Waking up beside him, cooking with him, hearing him laugh under his breath as I stole his coffee. It all just made sense.

And now it was almost over.

I knew what I had to do next. I stared at Dylan's name on the screen for what felt like a full minute.

Then I hit call.

It rang twice.

He answered on the third.

"Keira?" His voice was calm, but it had an edge to it. Like he wasn't sure if he should be relieved or upset.

I opened my mouth and tried to find something to say, but for a second, nothing came out.

Then finally, I said, "Hi."

There was a pause on his end. Just a beat too long.

"What the hell is going on? I've been trying to get a hold of you all day," he said.

"I know," I said softly. "I'm sorry. I just…needed some time."

Another pause.

"Are you okay?"

I looked down at the floor. My bare toes were pressed into the rug, cold from the tile. I wrapped the blanket tighter around my shoulders before answering.

"Yeah," I said. "I'm okay. Just tired."

"So that's what you're going with? Tired? You're staying with some guy I've never heard of, disappear for the entire day, and then use the tired excuse? I've been worried sick about you."

"I didn't mean to worry you," I said, and I meant it. I wasn't trying to be cruel. I just didn't know how to exist inside both parts of my life at once. "My phone's been off most of the day. I just needed the break."

"Jess called me," he said. "Said your flight might be rescheduled? That they're trying to move things around because of the storm?"

"Yeah, I just got off the phone with her," I said. "I'll be on a flight home tomorrow night. I guess they're going to postpone the tour until after the holidays."

"Okay," he said. "That's good. You'll be back soon then." The word "soon," landed heavy.

"Yeah, I'll keep you posted when I know more," I said finally.

"Alright." He hesitated. "And what about us?"

My throat tightened. I didn't know how to answer that. Not without lying. Not without saying too much. So I did what I always did when I didn't know how to explain what I was feeling. Deflect.

"I think I just need to get home," I said carefully. "We have a lot to talk about, but this isn't the time or the place."

"Okay," he said, a little quieter now. "Let me know what the plan is. I can pick you up from Logan tomorrow night, it doesn't matter what time it is. Just please answer my calls next time."

"Okay, I will. I promise."

The call ended, and the screen went dark in my hand.

I stared at it for a long time before I stood up, the blanket falling from my shoulders to the bed. The apartment was still quiet, except for the sounds of Miles in the kitchen filling the air.

I made my way back to where he was, trying to figure out what to do now.

Miles had his back to me, standing at the sink, washing the dishes. He took our mugs, which we had been using for the last two days, dried them off, and placed them in the cupboard.

I didn't want to say it.

I didn't want to be the one who shattered the peace we'd built over the last forty-eight hours, the version of us that had felt so good and real and simple for once. But the words were already pressing against the back of my throat.

So I picked up the book of matches on the counter and started lighting candles since the darkness was starting to fall outside.

"They got me on a flight," I said finally, voice low.

He stilled.

I watched his hand tighten slightly around the spoon he was cleaning. He didn't turn around.

"When?"

"Tomorrow night. Late."

He nodded once, then again, slower. "Right."

He kept his back to me. The silence stretched between us, long enough that I started to wonder if he was even going to say anything else. I waited. I gave him space. But when he turned around, I could see the effort it took him to keep his face still.

"So that's it?" he asked. "You're just going?"

I swallowed. "I don't want to. But I have to."

"You have to?"

His voice wasn't sharp. It wasn't cruel. But there was something tight behind it now.

Something cracking.

"I have responsibilities, Miles," I said carefully. "There are things I need to take care of back home. My book. The store. Dylan—"

He laughed, just once, but he wasn't amused. "Right. Dylan."

I stepped closer, folding my arms across my chest. "I'm not trying to hurt you."

"Then what are you doing?"

His eyes locked on mine, and for the first time all day, I felt the full weight of what he'd been holding back. All that hope he had inside of him. I had it too. It was right there. But I needed to take care of things first. There was so much to figure out, so much waiting for me back on the coast that I couldn't just ignore.

"What are *we* doing, Keira?" he asked. "Because it sure as hell doesn't feel casual."

"I don't know," I said finally, my voice barely above a whisper. "I don't have an answer for that yet."

His expression didn't change, but I saw something flicker behind his eyes. Something sharp and tired and disappointed. I hated it.

"I didn't come here planning for any of this to happen," I continued. "And I meant what I said. I don't regret it. I needed it. I needed you. But I can't just run away and hide here. Not without figuring everything else out first."

He shook his head slightly, like he didn't understand. "Figure what out? You either love someone or you don't."

"It's not that simple," I said. "I have a life back home. I have people who rely on me. A store to run. A book I'm supposed to be finishing. And yeah—Dylan. I owe it to him to at least face this honestly. To look him in the eyes and tell him it's over." I paused. "What about you? Are you going to quit your job without notice? Sell your condo? Move in with me? I'm not the only one who has decisions to make."

His jaw flexed. He walked over to me and cupped my face gently in his hands, his devastating blue eyes searching mine. "Do you love me?"

I stared at him, my heart pounding, every part of me feeling stretched too thin. "Yes."

"Then what else is there to figure out?" he asked, his voice low.

My eyes welled, tears threatening to break free. "Do you think this is easy for me?" I pulled back from his hands, my chest tight. "I need time," I said, softer now. "Time to think. To figure out what all of this means. I have a life I love, half a world away from here. Please, Miles. Just…try to understand. Be rational about this."

He just stood there, silent.

I hesitated for a second, then turned and walked toward the front door.

"Where are you going, Keira?" he called back to me.

"I just need some air. This is too much."

Our coats were still draped over the arm of the chair from the night we went out into the storm. I grabbed it, shoved my arms through the sleeves, and opened the door without looking back.

The cold air hit me the second I stepped outside, but I welcomed it. I closed the door gently behind me, walked down the front steps, and kept walking.

I didn't know where I was going.

I just knew I couldn't stay inside that apartment one second longer.

I walked for blocks without thinking.

The streets were mostly clear now, just a few patches of slush where the snow hadn't melted yet. The sidewalks, however, were still piled with snow. The cold didn't bother me. I barely felt it. I kept my hands shoved deep in my coat pockets, my head down, eyes focused on nothing in particular.

Everything inside me felt tight. My chest, my throat, the space between every breath. The pressure behind my eyes was building, and I didn't know how to stop it.

What Miles said...he wasn't wrong. But he wasn't fair, either.

I wasn't trying to run away from us. I was trying to give myself the space to choose him for real. Not out of nostalgia. Not out of comfort. Out of something deeper than the high of being in his arms after five years apart. I needed to go home and look at the life I spent years building before I could walk away from it.

I found a bench near the edge of a small neighborhood park and sat down, breathing hard like I'd been running even though I hadn't. My hands were shaking. I clenched them into fists inside my pockets.

The last forty-eight hours had been the best I'd felt in years. He breathed life back into me.

And somehow, I still felt like I was losing everything again.

I stared straight ahead as the night sky swallowed up the last of the sun. The air was crisp and dry. Now that the storm had mostly passed, people were out again walking dogs, carrying takeout, bundled in coats and scarves. Everyone moving through their own lives while mine felt like it had just split in two.

I don't know how long I sat there before I heard footsteps behind me slowing down. Then stopping.

I didn't need to turn around to know it was him.

He didn't say anything at first. Just stood there quietly, like he was waiting to see if I'd acknowledge him.

I didn't.

After a few seconds, he stepped forward and sat down beside me. His breath came out slowly, like he wasn't sure where to start.

"I'm sorry," he said quietly. "For acting the way I did."

I nodded, staring straight ahead.

"I just..." He let out a breath. "I don't want to lose you. I don't want you to walk away from me like I did to you. I can't go another five years without you, Keira."

That broke me. I turned to look at him, and this time, he was already watching me. His expression was calmer now. Sad and tired.

"I don't want to lose you either."

He looked down at the ground, then back at me again. "Then why do you have to go?"

I swallowed hard. "Because if I stay here without looking at everything else, I'll always wonder what I left unfinished. I'll always wonder if I made this choice too fast. And you don't deserve a version of me who still has questions hanging over her head."

He didn't argue with me.

He just nodded once. A quiet, reluctant kind of acceptance.

"I hate this. But I know you're right," he said.

Another silence passed between us. He shifted slightly, turning to face me more fully.

"I love you, Keira. I always have."

My chest cracked wide open.

"I love you too," I said as a tear finally escaped from me. "That's what makes this so hard."

After sitting in the silence for a while, Miles stood and offered me his hand. We walked back together, our fingers laced between us. When we got back to the apartment, we didn't bother with anything around us.

Everything was just as we'd left it. A few plates still in the sink, candles burning down to the end of their wicks, blankets strewn across the floor in the living room, but neither of us made a move to clean up.

Instead, we went straight to the bedroom.

I changed into something more comfortable. He pulled off his sweater and crawled beneath the blankets, leaving space for me like he always used to. I slipped in beside him, and he pulled me in without hesitation, my head settling against his chest, one of his hands resting on the small of my back.

We didn't try to sleep right away.

Instead, we lay there in the dark, legs tangled, the air between us lighter than it had been all night. I rested my head against his chest, listening to the steady sound of his heartbeat beneath my ear, and I didn't move when his fingers started tracing slow, absent shapes along my spine.

We talked in soft voices. "I still remember the night you fell asleep on my shoulder in the backseat of Seth's car," he said after a while. "You'd been teasing me about the entire bucket of popcorn I spilled at the theatre, and then ten minutes later, you were completely out. Dead weight."

I laughed quietly. "In my defense, it was late. And the movie was boring."

"It was *The Dark Knight*."

"Exactly."

He chuckled, the sound low in his chest. "You drooled on my sweatshirt."

"Oh, you're so full of shit." I couldn't help but laugh at that because he was absolutely right, but there was no way I was admitting that.

We fell quiet for a moment until I spoke again. "Do you remember my sixteenth birthday?"

"You mean Lexi's surprise party that you almost ruined because you hated being late for anything?"

I smiled into his shirt. "I had a feeling something was up. But I didn't expect you to be there since you were staying at your grandparents' place on the Cape."

"You looked like you were about to cry when you saw me."

"I was. The surprise of you being there was better than the actual party." He didn't say anything. Just pulled me a little closer.

We kept going, letting the memories drift out like they'd been waiting all this time to be spoken about again.

The nights we snuck out of our cabins at camp to sit by the old fire pit and smoke cigarettes like we were cool, talking for hours with our knees brushing and the stars overhead.

All the concerts we went to together: cheap tickets, long drives, getting caught in the rain on the way out of one in Connecticut.

Our weekend trips to New York City, and how he always let me choose where we ate, even when it meant walking twenty blocks to get some overpriced pasta I found online.

And perhaps one of my favorite memories, the time we found our way to some random basement auction in the backwoods of Massachusetts, way past dark. I had bid on a vintage radio and won. I was so happy that night.

And then there were all the times it almost happened.

The nights we ended up in the same bed, the same sleeping bag, the same parked car. The two of us slipping away from a friend's party to steal kisses on the back porch, hidden in the dark. Our hands tangled, kissing, touching, loving each other without saying it.

Something silent, always holding us back.

The almosts that started to stack up over the years. More than friends, never quite more than that. Too afraid to take the chance.

"It was always there," he said after a long stretch of silence. "Even when we didn't talk about it."

I nodded against him. "I know."

Another pause.

"We were basically always together," he said. "We just didn't know what to do with it."

"I still don't," I whispered.

His hand stilled against my back. "We've got time."

Eventually, our breathing slowed, our bodies sinking deeper into the mattress. My arm rested over his chest. His chin rested against the top of my head.

And that's how we fell asleep.

Still holding each other.

Still holding on.

Chapter 20

PRESENT DAY

CHICAGO, ILLINOIS

The next morning, we kept things simple and had gone out to pick up some groceries to make breakfast together. We didn't talk about the flight. We didn't talk about what came next. We just moved slowly, talking about anything else we could think of, like if we stretched the morning long enough, the rest of it wouldn't have to come.

We left the apartment a few hours early.

We stopped at her hotel first. She already had the key tucked into the front pocket of the coat she'd been borrowing the last couple of days.

Neither of us said much as we walked through the lobby and took the elevator up. I kept glancing at her as we stood side by side in the mirrored wall, her face calm but unreadable, like she was trying to hold everything together until she was back in the privacy of her own home.

The room, I assumed, was exactly as she left it, with folded towels, a single suitcase by the window, and the bed made thanks to the housekeepers. It felt untouched, like time had paused here while the rest of the world moved on. She walked in first, dropped the coat on the chair, and stood still for a few seconds like she wasn't sure where to start.

I stayed near the door, watching her.

She knelt beside the suitcase, unzipped it, and began packing slowly. Methodically. Clothes she barely wore this week. Toiletries she lined up in the bathroom but never touched. A notebook. A folded itinerary. The little signs of a life she was supposed to be living.

She didn't look at me, and I didn't interrupt her. I just sat on the edge of the bed and watched her move through the room like she didn't recognize any of it.

And that's when it hit me that she was right. Everything had changed in only a matter of days. She needed to go back home and figure out her life. And I needed to figure out mine.

When she reached for a sweater that had slipped off the chair, her hands lingered on the fabric a second longer than necessary. She folded it carefully and placed it on top of the rest of her clothes.

The suitcase was small, just a standard black roller bag she'd had for years. I remembered it from old trips to the train station, from the back of my car more times than I could count.

It was worn in at the edges, and one side of the zipper was starting to fray. It looked exactly the same, but now, I hated the sight of it. Because it meant that this time, she was the one leaving.

When she finally zipped it closed, she stood there with her hand resting on the handle. Her shoulders dropped. Her face was still. But I could feel how much this was hurting her.

"You ready?" I asked.

She nodded without looking at me. "Yeah."

And even though I knew it was inevitable, it still didn't feel real.

We drove to the airport in silence. She sat beside me in the passenger seat with her legs crossed and her hands folded in her lap.

Every so often, I'd feel her eyes on me, like she was waiting for me to say something. Anything. I didn't look back. I wasn't sure I could.

By the time I pulled into the departures lane, my hands were clenched tight around the steering wheel. Her flight wasn't delayed. No last-minute storm. No act of God to buy us more time.

After helping her with her bag, I stood there with my hands in my pockets, trying not to look like I was falling apart. Just admiring how beautiful she was and trying as hard as I could to burn that beauty into my brain.

She turned to me. Her eyes were glassy, her lips slightly parted like she was still searching for the right words.

"I really hate this," she whispered.

I nodded. "Me too."

She looked down, swallowed hard, then looked back up at me. "I just need time. That's all this is. I need to go home and figure things out. Sort through what's real and what's not and...I can't do that here."

"I know."

"I'm not choosing him," she said.

That hit something inside me I hadn't been prepared for.

She continued. "But I need to salvage the mess I made. For him. And for me. And...for you." I couldn't speak. My throat felt tight. My chest was burning.

She reached out, wrapped her arms around my neck, and pulled me in. I held her like I didn't care who saw us. Like I didn't care that this felt like the last time.

"I love you," she whispered against my shoulder.

"I love you too."

She pulled back, brushing a tear from her cheek with the back of her hand.

"Please don't forget this," she said.

"I couldn't if I tried."

She held my face in her hands for a second, her eyes full of something close to panic, then she squeezed them shut and turned toward the security line.

I watched her the entire time. I didn't look away as she handed over her ID, as she placed her bag on the conveyor belt, as she stepped out of her boots and walked barefoot across the cold airport floor.

She looked over her shoulder, giving me a small smile that made my heart tighten, then lifted her hand in a soft wave before she rounded the corner toward the gates.

When she finally disappeared from view, I stood there for another minute, staring at the empty space where she'd been.

Then I turned and walked back to the car.

I got in, shut the door, and just sat there with my hands resting on the steering wheel. The terminal windows glowed above me, the buzz of travel and movement all around, but inside the car, it was silent.

A single tear ran down my cheek, and then another. I didn't wipe them away.

Because sitting there alone, in the middle of the god damn departures lane, I realized something I'd been too afraid to admit until now.

This time, it really felt like goodbye.

And I didn't know how to live with that.

Chapter 21

KEIRA

PRESENT DAY

ROCKPORT, MASSACHUSETTS

It had been two weeks since I saw him.

Fourteen days since I stood in that airport and walked away without looking back. Fourteen days since I told him I needed time. Since I told myself I was doing the right thing. That I couldn't stay.

I hadn't heard from him since.

No texts. No calls. No check-ins.

I told him I needed space, and he gave it to me. And I was okay with that, for now.

The shop was closed for the afternoon. I'd pulled the curtain across the front door and turned off the "Open" sign sometime around lunch. Not because I had anywhere to be, but because I couldn't keep pretending to be okay for customers today. I didn't want to make small talk about book club picks or gift wrap another paperback for someone who still believed love was simple, all because the other romance writers had written it that way. We were all fooling ourselves.

I was on the floor in the back corner of the shop, Lola asleep by my side, surrounded by half-filled notebooks, pens scattered across the rug, and my laptop open beside me, its screen dark from inactivity.

There were sticky notes stuck to the wall behind me, pieces of paper taped to the front of the bookshelf, loose outlines and titles and scenes scribbled in quick, desperate handwriting.

My eyes started to burn from staring at blank pages. I'd been at it for hours. Trying to force something onto the page. Trying to come up with anything that felt honest. Real. My publishing house expected a novel from me in four months, and nothing was working. I was screwed.

I leaned back against the shelf and pulled my knees up to my chest, staring at the clutter around me. Coffee gone cold in my usual mug. A playlist was still looping softly through the speakers overhead. My fingers were stained with ink from a pen that had leaked earlier, and I could still feel the tension in my jaw from clenching it too long.

My thoughts were stuck in the same loop.

What was he doing right now?

Was he at work? At home? Was he sleeping okay? Was someone else keeping him company at night? Had he finally stopped checking his phone every time it buzzed?

Because I hadn't.

Even when I promised myself I wouldn't, I still glanced down every time my phone lit up, hoping for something from him. Even just a single word. Some sign that he hadn't closed the door all the way.

But there was nothing.

Just silence. And all the space I said I needed.

I lowered my forehead to my knees and closed my eyes, breathing slow, trying to quiet everything screaming inside of me.

I didn't know how to write a love story when my ending still felt undecided.

I didn't even know how to begin.

*****

THEN — TWO WEEKS AGO

When I got home, the apartment didn't feel like mine anymore.

It was the same as I left it. The lights were still off. The framed photo of Dylan and me still sat on the hallway table beside a vase of dried flowers. My boots were lined up neatly by the door where I'd left them. Lola greeted me at the door with plenty of kisses. Nothing had changed.

But everything felt different.

I rolled my suitcase inside and stood there with my hand still on the doorknob, staring into the living room. The couch looked untouched. The throw blanket perfectly folded. The kitchen was clean. Dylan's keys were still in the bowl beside mine. There was a grocery list on the fridge that I barely remembered writing.

Dylan trailed in behind me.

When he picked me up from the airport, he didn't try to kiss me. He didn't ask about the trip. He sat in silence and waited for me to start.

And I told him the truth.

I told him I loved him in a way that was safe and comfortable, but no longer enough. I told him I had spent the last year trying to write about love without really feeling it, and that I didn't want to live like that anymore. I told him I wasn't coming back just to pick up where we left off. I told him he deserved more than I could give him, that living with me wasn't fair to him.

He didn't yell. He didn't argue. He just sat there with his hands folded and his jaw locked, listening to every word like he already knew it was coming. I think in a way, he felt the same.

When I finished, he looked at me for a long time before he finally spoke. "Is there someone else?"

I paused, then answered honestly. "There's someone I gave my heart to a very long time ago. And I never asked for it back."

That was the only time he looked away.

"I just want you to be happy, Keira," he had said. "However that's achieved."

We decided to break off the engagement, and he moved out the next day. I told him that I wished him well. I wanted him to find someone he deserved. I told him I was sorry. I had treated him badly, and he didn't deserve that. He had given me more grace than I'd earned, and the least I could do was tell the truth and let him go without any more confusion.

Jess came over that night with wine and a charcuterie board she didn't bother to plate. She just threw the wrapped cheeses and crackers onto the cutting board and kicked her shoes off at the door like she'd been waiting for this conversation all week.

We sat on the living room floor with the coffee table pulled close between us, and for the first time since I'd come home, I let myself fall apart.

I told her everything, tears flowing down my face.

About Chicago. About the book event. About the moment I saw him at the shop, and the way it knocked the air out of me.

I told her about the days we spent holed up in his apartment, about the storm, about the snowball fight, about the morning I woke up in his bed and didn't want to be anywhere else.

I told her I still loved him. That I always had.

She didn't interrupt. She just poured another glass and nodded like she'd been waiting for me to say those words out loud since the day Dylan proposed.

We talked for hours. About how long I'd been holding myself back. Like I was living in the space between what I had and what I really wanted. How it felt like all I was doing was waiting for something real to begin. How I wasn't proud of the way I'd acted, and

I wanted to do things right. I didn't want to start a relationship on the betrayal of someone else

When she finally left just after midnight, I sat on the couch with Lola curled up next to me, the wine half-drunk and the room spinning slightly around me. I looked over at the blank wall where Dylan's framed art had once hung, now gone. There was an emptiness there that should've scared me.

But it didn't.

It felt honest. Like a space that was finally ready to be filled with something real.

***

I stretched my legs out in front of me, then pushed myself up off the floor. My knees cracked when I stood. The lights in the shop were dim, the front curtain still drawn, casting everything in a muted gray. I moved slowly through the aisles, brushing my fingers along the shelves as I walked, not really looking for anything, just needing to move.

Halfway down the second row, I paused in front of the poetry section. It wasn't one I usually spent much time in. I kept it stocked mostly for the regulars who asked, like the college kids, old women, or the occasional romantic passing through town. But something drew me to it today.

I crouched down and pulled out a small, pale blue paperback. One of the indie titles I'd picked up at a conference last year.

The cover was soft and understated, and the spine was barely cracked. I turned it over in my hands, then brought it back with me to the circle I created on the floor.

Before sitting down, I grabbed a matchbook from the drawer behind the counter and lit a few of the short pillar candles I kept scattered around the space. One by the register, one near the window, one right beside me on the floor. The scent was faint with patchouli, my favorite, and it helped take the edge off the stillness.

I sat cross-legged with the book in my lap, flipping through pages without much focus. The poems were short, some no more than a line or two. Most of them didn't land. But then, tucked about a third of the way in, I stopped.

Just one line. Centered on the page, printed in small, even type.

Sometimes I wonder if we would've made it if one of us had just come back.

I stared at it.

Then I read it again.

And again. And again.

I felt something sharp tighten in my chest.

Because it was us. All of it. Me and Miles. Every missed moment, every goodbye, every almost that led us back to now.

And suddenly, it was here. Right in front of me.

The story I'd been trying to find. Not fiction. Not a perfect romance tied up with a bow. But something real. Messy and flawed and unfinished.

I grabbed the nearest notebook and opened it to a blank page.

At the top, I wrote: *If You Ever Come Back*

And for the first time in weeks, my hand didn't stop moving.

I filled five pages before I even realized I was hungry. Another ten before I looked at the clock and saw it was nearly 3 a.m. I slept on the couch with the notebook still in my lap and a pen tucked behind my ear, a candle burned down to a stub beside me.

The next morning, I opened the shop late, and only because I had to. I kept the register running, but didn't make eye contact with anyone who came in. I spent every free second behind the counter typing what I'd written by hand the night before, then starting fresh again as soon as I was done. I didn't tell Jess what I was working on. I wanted to keep this my personal project for now.

For the first time in months, I felt present. Awake. Like I wasn't trying to be someone else for anyone.

The story came faster than I expected. Not because it was easy, but because it was honest. Because I wasn't fabricating a plot or creating characters from scratch. I was telling the truth. The ugly parts. The beautiful parts. The parts I never let myself say out loud.

It started with camp. With the summer when everything changed. With the way Miles looked at me before I even knew what it meant to be loved like that.

It moved through our firsts and our almosts, the late-night calls and the long silences, the missed chances and the moments I wanted to take back. I didn't soften the endings. I didn't protect myself from the worst of it. I wrote what happened.

And then I wrote what it felt like.

Jess started covering extra shifts at the shop without me asking. She showed up with coffee every morning and checked in only to make sure I was eating.

Some days, she sat beside me while I wrote, reading quietly or scrolling through her phone without speaking. Other days, I didn't see her at all.

I stayed holed up in the back room with my laptop, a blanket, and mugs full of coffee or tea that always went cold before I finished them.

The apartment changed too. Once Dylan's things were gone, I rearranged the living room. I got rid of the table he loved, the lamp I never liked. I took our photos down. Not out of anger, but out of necessity. I couldn't write this story surrounded by a life that didn't fit anymore.

There were days I doubted myself. Days the words didn't come, or I hated every sentence I wrote. But I kept going. I went to bed thinking about the book and woke up reaching for it. I dreamed scenes and dialogue. I kept a notepad by the shower. I stayed up until two, three, four in the morning, rereading, deleting, rewriting again.

It wasn't about getting it perfect. It was about getting it right.

Two months passed like that.

And then one day, I finished it.

It wasn't a dramatic moment. No tears, no music swelling, no thunderstorm outside the window. I typed the final line and just...sat there. My hands stilled on the keys. My breathing was a little unsteady.

Then I saved the file, closed my laptop, and filled a large glass of red wine to the top. I took a bubble bath, downed the glass and passed out into the deepest sleep I have had in recent months.

I sent it off the next morning before I could second-guess myself. Just a short email to my agent, the manuscript attached, no explanation needed. I didn't bother writing a pitch or a blurb. I didn't try to summarize what it was about. If she wanted to read it, she would.

Then I shut my laptop and sat on my hands, because if I didn't, I knew I'd email her again.

Or worse, call her.

The first few days of waiting were manageable. I cleaned the apartment. Caught up on rest. Walked along the shoreline near the harbor just to get some air in my lungs. Jess kept checking in. She made me go out to dinner with her, just once, to remind me I was still human.

But by the second week, the silence got heavier.

I started pacing more. Picking up my phone every ten minutes. Refreshing my email constantly, even though I knew nothing would change. I told myself it was fine—that this was normal. That she was probably just busy. That there was nothing I could do but wait.

Still, every time the inbox refreshed, and her name wasn't there, my chest tightened a little more.

By week three, I stopped sleeping. Not because I was anxious, exactly, but because my mind wouldn't stop running. I kept replaying the scenes I'd written. Wondering if I'd said too much. Or not enough. If I'd made a mistake putting it all down the way I did.

And then, out of nowhere, she called.

"Keira," she said before I could even speak. "I finished it."

I froze, one hand still resting on the register drawer.

"You finished it?"

"All in one sitting," she said. "I couldn't stop! Sorry it took so long for me to get back to you."

I swallowed. "And?"

There was a pause. Then she said, "It's the most honest thing you've ever written. The rawest. The most human. It's good. Really good. It's real and relatable. Something that people want—no—need out of a romance novel."

I didn't know what to say. My throat was tight, my heart pounding so hard I thought she might hear it through the phone.

"We're moving fast on this one," she continued. "I already sent it to the house and your editor. We're planning to print by the end of the month. Expect proofs soon."

I blinked. "Wait. You're publishing it?"

She laughed kindly. "Keira. We're publishing the hell out of it."

That was when it hit me.

Not just that it was going to be a real book. But that someone else believed in it. That someone had read all the broken pieces I'd laid out on the page and still thought it was worth putting out into the world.

When the call ended, I set the phone down and lowered myself to the floor behind the counter. Same spot where I'd started it all. Same silence. Same walls.

But this time, I wasn't stuck.

I knew where I was going and who I was writing for.

***

MONTHS LATER — JUNE

LOGAN AIRPORT, BOSTON, MASSACHUSETTS

It still didn't feel real most days.

One month on shelves. One month of interviews and press, and tagged photos that I could barely keep up with. One month of readers crying online over lines I wrote at three in the morning with a blanket wrapped around my shoulders and my laptop balanced on my knees. *If You Ever Come Back* wasn't just out…it was everywhere. Somehow, in the swirl of book clubs and blogs and airport bookstores, it had climbed its way to the top of the New York Times list in its first week. And stayed there.

I sat alone at Gate 23, one leg crossed over the other, a coffee going cold beside me, and my phone face down on my thigh. I wasn't on a tour. Not officially. That wouldn't pick back up until the fall. Instead, I was heading back to Chicago. Back to The Oak and Sage Bookshop for a signing. I was heading back to find him.

The airport was loud and full of kids arguing with parents, flight announcements echoing every few minutes, the constant screech of suitcase wheels, but inside my head, everything was quiet. Still. It had been that way ever since I hit send on that final manuscript months ago. Like something inside me had finally settled.

And still, even with the calm, I couldn't stop thinking about him.

Going into an airport from here on out would always remind me of Chicago. Of the day I left. Of the way his hands hovered near mine like he didn't want to let go. Of the look on his face when I said I needed time. Of how I'd held him just before I left, thinking, "Please, God, don't let this be the last time I see him."

But then I wrote the book.

And part of me still believed he'd read it.

I didn't know if that was foolish or brave. But I believed it anyway.

I told my agent to set me up in Chicago for the first signing since the release. I was excited to go back, but I also couldn't shake the possible fear of rejection. What if it was too late? I still hadn't spoken to Miles since I left Chicago. He had no idea I was coming. I didn't have a plan, just faith in this story reaching him, in myself, in us.

The boarding announcement came over the speaker, and I stood, sliding my phone into my bag and grabbing my tote.

There was nothing flashy about this trip. No event coordinator waiting on the other end. No driver holding a sign with my name. Just me, a bestselling book tucked into my carry-on and a signing table with my name on a printed card.

And also, the faint hope that maybe, somehow, he'd show up.

But I didn't let myself think too hard about that.

I just walked toward the gate. One step. Then another. Steadily toward whatever came next.

Chapter 22

MILES

THEN — MAY

CHICAGO, ILLINOIS

I passed the Oak and Sage on my way home more often than I cared to admit. I never meant to. It wasn't on my usual route. But ever since she left, my steps seemed to pull me this way without thinking.

The first time it happened, I told myself it was a coincidence. The second time, I pretended I just liked the side streets better. But by the third or fourth time, I stopped pretending altogether. I walked past it because it reminded me of her. Because for a few seconds, even just in passing, it felt like being close to something that still had her in it.

I missed her in a way that didn't always make sense. It was quiet. Constant. Woven into everything. I saw her in the sunlight on the sidewalk, in storefront windows, in the faces of strangers passing by.

I didn't know if she was coming back. I didn't even know if she should. But I knew one thing with absolute certainty: no matter what happened, I was never going to stop loving her.

And then, just as that thought settled, I saw it.

In the front window, just above a little wooden sign and a scattering of flower petals, was a display of new releases. In the center of a round table and propped up on a wooden easel, surrounded by copies arranged like a heart, was her name.

Keira Sullivan, *If You Ever Come Back*

I didn't move, and for a few seconds, I stopped breathing.

The cover was simple. Soft blues and warm whites. Her name was in bold serif. I stepped closer, pressing a hand to the glass without thinking. Her book. The one she couldn't write.

It was here. In my city. On this street. It existed. And somehow, I hadn't known.

I pushed open the door before I could talk myself out of it. The little bell above the entrance chimed, and the scent of paper and leather wrapped around me.

The clerk behind the counter looked up with a polite smile. "Hi there. Can I help you find something?"

I didn't look away from the display. "Yeah," I said, already moving toward it. "That one."

She laughed. "Good choice. It's been flying off the shelves since release day."

"I didn't even know it was out," I muttered, more to myself than to her.

As she rang it up, she added, "If you're a fan, she's going to be here next month doing a signing. June fifteenth. Should be a great event. We've had the pleasure of hosting her once before, and she's just wonderful!"

I stared at the book in my hand that now belonged to me. "Yeah," I replied. "She is."

My stomach turned. I paid in cash and walked out with the book clutched tight in my hand.

***

I couldn't wait. I didn't even take off my coat or check my email or put on music. As soon as I stepped through the door of my apartment, I sat down on the couch and started reading.

I read the first five chapters before I even blinked. It was like having the breath knocked out of me. Not because the writing was good—which of course it was—but because it was her. Her voice, her timing, her humor, her sadness. Her heart, right there in the pages. She wasn't trying to impress anyone. She wasn't trying to be clever. She was just telling the truth.

By the time I hit chapter ten, I was crying, quiet tears slipping down my face without warning. Because every scene brought me back. Every line held something that was a part of our life, and I felt like she was speaking directly to me.

She did change the names of the characters, but she didn't hide behind them. To others, it was fiction, but only she and I knew better. She wrote our story. All the flaws, all the love, and all the heartbreak.

I called in sick the next morning. And the one after that.

I didn't move much. I barely ate. I didn't talk to anyone. I just read. Slowly. Carefully.

Letting every single word find a home inside me.

The camp memories. The night of the storm. Our near misses. She remembered everything. She saw everything. She'd always been watching, just like I had. And now it was all right here. Undeniable.

When I turned the final page, I didn't move for a long time.

The room was quiet. My coffee was cold. My eyes burned.

I set the book down gently on the table like it was something sacred. I'd never felt anything like it.

She had written the most beautiful thing I'd ever read, and I didn't know what to do now in this moment, but I knew one thing for certain.

I was going to that signing.

And this time, I wasn't going to let her walk away.

Chapter 23

KIERA

PRESENT DAY

CHICAGO, ILLINOIS

The plane touched down just after seven. The sky was overcast, but warm and heavy with that early summer stillness that settles before a storm. Or after one.

As the car drove silently through the streets and the city moved past the windows, I couldn't stop myself from wondering if he knew I was here. I tried to keep my mind from wandering at all, but it was difficult to help.

The hotel was small and tucked off a quieter street, not far from the Oak and Sage Bookshop. I hadn't wanted anything extravagant. Just space. A bed, a desk, and a bathtub deep enough to disappear into for a little while, and luckily, this room had all three.

I dropped my bag at the foot of the bed without unpacking. My shoes came off first, then my jacket, then the necklace I'd been fidgeting with for the entire flight.

I moved slowly through the room, flipping on lights, checking the temperature, and laying out clothes for the morning. It was automatic, ritualistic really, but nothing made me feel settled. My chest was tight. My thoughts were spinning. I needed to come down from whatever this was before I burned out completely.

The tub took time to fill. I poured in the lavender bubble soak Jess had stuffed into my suitcase and let the scent settle around me. I didn't check my phone. I didn't bring a book. I just stepped in and let the heat bleed into my limbs.

It helped, but only a little. I was still an anxious mess.

I lay my head back and stared at the ceiling, arms resting on the sides, water licking up past my collarbones. I was exhausted, but my mind wouldn't slow down. I kept running through every possible outcome of tomorrow. What if no one came? What if too many did?

What if he doesn't show up? Do I go to his apartment?

The not knowing was worse than any answer.

I sank lower into the water, eyes closed, trying to block it all out, but nothing worked. The nerves weren't just about seeing him. They were about being seen. Really seen.

There would be people there tomorrow who'd read things I've never said out loud. Strangers who felt like they knew me. And maybe now they would. That was the scariest part.

Eventually, when the water turned lukewarm, and the bubbles thinned to a film, I pulled myself out and wrapped up in one of the thick hotel towels. I brushed my teeth. Pulled on a worn t-shirt. Turned off all but one light. I stood at the window for a while, arms crossed, forehead against the cool glass.

The city was still alive outside. Lights flickering, cars moving slowly beneath me. I wondered if he ever walked down that street. If he ever looked up and thought about me the way I thought about him.

I crawled into bed but didn't reach for my phone. I didn't want updates or texts or reminders. I just wanted sleep. Real, deep sleep. But I knew I wouldn't get it.

Not tonight.

Not with the possibility of seeing him again hanging just on the other side of morning.

The signing started at noon. By 11:15 a.m., the shop was already at capacity.

The moment I stepped through the back entrance and caught sight of the crowd, my stomach turned. People were packed shoulder to shoulder, a line that wrapped from the register to the back wall. I caught glimpses of people holding copies of the book close to their chests, as if it meant something to them. I could see the creases in the covers, with bookmarks sticking out, notes probably scribbled in the margins.

I tried to breathe through it. This was a good thing. The best thing. The event manager from the store whispered that we'd sold out of every single copy before the doors even opened.

They'd turned off the online RSVPs two days ago. People were still lining up outside.

It was twice the size of the Rockport launch. Maybe more.

I smiled. I signed. I posed for pictures. I listened to a girl cry as she explained how the book helped her tell her best friend she had feelings for him, and how he had felt the same. I held the hand of a boy who said the ending made him call his ex just to say sorry. I was grateful and overwhelmed by it all. The kind of overwhelmed that doesn't hit until much later, when it's quiet again.

But through it all, I kept looking.

Each time the door opened. Each time someone stepped out of line. Each time someone laughed or ducked behind a display.

I kept scanning for him.

But he hadn't shown.

The disappointment was sharp and hot in the back of my throat, but buried quickly. I had work to do. People to thank. A room full of readers who deserved more than my personal ghosts.

Still, the longer it went, the heavier it sat in my chest. Maybe he wasn't coming. Maybe he'd read the book and closed the door on us for good. Maybe I'd just completely embarrassed myself, and this was the price of putting the truth on the page—having no control over how someone else receives it.

Eventually, they cleared space and set up the mic stand for the Q&A. It was nothing formal, just like last time. We were tucked in the back room with a few rows of folding chairs and the rest of the crowd standing wherever they could fit. I took a sip of water, sat down, and folded my hands in my lap.

The questions started simple.

"What inspired the structure of the novel?"

"How did it feel to publish something so personal?"

"Will there be a sequel?"

I answered them all, honestly and carefully.

The event was winding down, and the window was closing. I had just about given up thinking he would show, hanging my head in clear disappointment.

Then, the mic was passed to another person, and a voice broke through.

"I have a question."

My heart stopped.

Not because of the words, but because of who they belonged to.

The voice came from the back, behind the seated rows. It was unmistakable.

I looked up.

And there, standing with the mic in his hand, was Miles.

He stood just inside the door, one hand in his pocket, a copy of my book tucked under his arm. He looked tired. Like he hadn't slept since he finished reading it. Like it had wrecked him.

Like he let it.

Our eyes locked.

226

And the entire room disappeared.

He took one step forward. Then another. His smile was soft and a little nervous. Like this wasn't easy for him, but he was doing it anyway.

"So, she said if she ever came back, she'd be there to stay. She'd be his for good..." he said, lifting the book slightly in his hand, thumb tucked into the page. "So... did she?"

The room held still. People glanced at one another. Some confused. Some were already catching on. I could feel the tension in the air start to shift, pressurized and expectant.

And then he said it. "Did she ever come back?"

He said it like a question he already knew the answer to. Like a line lifted straight from the ending of the book.

He smiled, just slightly, and my heart broke open in my chest.

I didn't speak. I didn't say a word. But my breath hitched.

I stood up from the folding chair I had been sitting in and moved straight through the crowd.

It parted around me like instinct. Like everyone already knew where I was going. The world had narrowed down to this one path. This one moment.

Him.

And when I reached him, I didn't hesitate.

I dropped my hands to his face, leaned in, and kissed him deep and sure, right there in front of everyone. His hands came around my waist, holding me like he'd waited years to do it.

The crowd erupted behind us with overlapping clapping, laughing, and cheering. There had been a few people gasping and whispering, "Oh my god, that's him. That's who the book was about."

Some people cried. Someone said, "I knew it."

Flashes went off. Phones lifted. A reader nearby muttered, "This is better than the ending of the book."

I heard it all, but didn't at the same time. It was muted, as if we were underwater.

And besides, I was too busy kissing him.
Kissing him because he was here. Because he read it.
Because he came back.
And because I finally did too.

Epilogue

KIERA

CHRISTMAS — 6 MONTHS LATER

MANCHESTER-BY-THE-SEA, MASSACHUSETTS

The house sat just off a narrow winding road, halfway up a small hill overlooking the ocean. It was a two-story colonial with weathered shingles, white trim, and a wraparound porch that made it feel like somewhere you never wanted to leave. A place where roots grew. It was older, but solid. The hardwood floors creaked in a few places. The windows stuck if you didn't open them the right way. But it was ours.

We'd spent the fall painting the walls, replacing the light fixtures, picking out rugs and bookshelves, and a proper desk for my writing loft upstairs. It finally felt like home.

We each had places to go during the day. Miles would commute to his new office in Boston, while I was upstairs in the office we built on the second floor of the house. And at the end of the day, we both ended up here, together. Always.

I sold the apartment and shop in Rockport shortly after we

moved. In town, I found a small retail space just off the main street. It wasn't anything flashy, but was been warm and inviting.

I turned it into the new bookshop. It didn't take long for it to find its rhythm. Business was steady, and every time a new shipment of my novels came in, the shelves emptied by the end of the week. People liked that the author worked behind the counter. I liked it too. It made everything feel personal.

Lola adjusted easily. She had her spot in the sunroom and a trail she ran every morning along the edge of the fence. Winter—our Corgi—took a little longer.

She was smaller, quieter, more cautious at first. But she followed Lola everywhere and eventually warmed up. We adopted her in October, the same day as the first snowfall here on the coast. Miles had picked her out. He had said that Lola could use some company and that we needed something to mark the shift in our lives. We named her Winter as a reminder of the time that brought us back together.

It was Christmas Eve, a full year since the last time everything changed.

I woke up, pulled on a sweatshirt, and headed downstairs. He was already in the kitchen, barefoot, making pancakes. The dogs were hovering nearby, hoping some scraps would fall.

"Morning," he said, looking over his shoulder at me.

"Good morning, you." I stepped beside him and leaned against the counter.

He poured another circle of batter onto the pan. "I used the cinnamon you like and made you a London Fog," he said, handing me a warm mug of it.

I smiled. "Thank you."

We didn't rush. Breakfast was slow. Simple. He made the coffee. I sliced strawberries. We ate in the dining nook by the windows and talked about the plans for tomorrow.

Christmas Day with our families in Portland would consist of an early drive and dinner with both of our families at my childhood home. We'd done Thanksgiving with Jess and Beth, so this felt like the right way to close the year.

I'd heard through the grapevine that Dylan had met someone. They'd eloped and, according to Jess, were expecting a baby soon. Jess had flashed me a picture of the couple on her phone. The way his wife looked at him warmed my heart. After the way I'd treated him, I was truly glad he'd found someone who loved him the way he deserved to be loved.

After we cleaned up, we bundled up and walked the dogs through town, hand in hand, as we did most mornings. It was cold but not too cold.

Most of the shops along the main street were still closed, their windows frosted over and dark, but a few glowed softly with twinkle lights left on overnight. A local bakery had its door propped open, the smell of cinnamon and fresh bread spilling out into the cold morning air. We passed a woman cradling a paper bag against her chest, steam rising from the top, and a man carrying a stack of neatly wrapped gifts under one arm, his scarf trailing behind him in the wind.

The town was wrapped in a quiet that comes only early in the morning, with snow-dusted rooftops, the caw of distant gulls, and the simple rhythm of life along the coast.

The day moved slowly, but I liked it that way. Everything about our life felt steady now. Not perfect, but secure.

Our dogs tugged a little on their leashes as we walked back up the hill toward our house. We talked about the future: his firm continuing to grow, my next book, and maybe a trip in the spring somewhere warm or tropical. I told him I wanted to start a small writing group at the bookshop in town. He told me he thought that was a good idea. He always supported and encouraged me, and I was so grateful for that.

Our life had become everything I hoped it would be. It was

comfortable and full of the kind of love that was never questioned. That night, we curled up on the couch with the dogs, a bowl of popcorn between us, and put on *Gremlins*, the Christmas movie we used to watch every year as kids. It still held up.

As we watched, I couldn't help but admire our little corner of the world. A fresh pine garland was draped over the mantle, woven with tiny golden lights and dried orange slices, filling the room with a faint citrus and evergreen scent. The tree stood near the front window, modest in size but lovingly decorated with handmade ornaments, a few mismatched baubles, and a star that leaned slightly to the left.

There were candles on every surface, flickering softly, casting a golden glow over worn bookshelves and plush throw blankets draped over the couch. A record player sat quietly in the corner, a stack of all our favorite albums beside it. In the kitchen, a plate of half-eaten cookies rested near a steaming mug. It all looked lived-in and loved-in. It had become our home.

Outside, the neighborhood was quiet. Inside, everything felt warm and festive. I knew tomorrow would be a lot since it was our first time seeing both sides of our family together in years, but for now, we let ourselves just enjoy the calm. We stayed like that for hours, drifting in and out of sleep until the tree lights dimmed on their timer and the dogs finally stopped begging for snacks.

When we finally made it upstairs, I crawled into bed next to him and felt something I hadn't felt in years.

Peace.

***

We made it to Portland a little after ten the next morning. The drive wasn't bad. Just over an hour up the coast with Winter curled in the backseat and Lola's head resting on the console.

We'd packed everything the night before. All the gifts, dog beds, and a tin of sugar cookies Miles had insisted on baking himself were ready to go, so the morning had been on easy mode.

When we pulled up to my parents' house, the driveway was already full. A wreath hung on the door, and the smell of cinnamon and roasted ham wafted through the air before we even stepped inside.

My mom wrapped me in a hug the second we walked through the door.

"There she is," she said, holding on a little longer than usual. "I've been waiting for this Christmas for years."

I laughed, surprised. "For years?"

She pulled back, giving me a look that told me not to play dumb. "Oh, please. You think I didn't know? I've known since you were fifteen, and you would blush every time he looked at you. I used to tell myself it would happen when it was supposed to. And now here we are."

Miles rolled his eyes in the background, but he smiled too. There was no hiding how much it meant to him. "I'm just glad you approve, Carol."

"I always approved of you Miles."

My mother drove me crazy most days, but it warmed me to hear her talk about him like that.

Inside, the house was warm and full, with his sister Emma, who had flown in from Denver, and her two kids were already running through the living room with bits of wrapping paper stuck to their shoes.

We spent the late morning exchanging gifts, passing plates of food, and sitting around the tree telling stories. My mom brought out photo albums, and Emma kept trying to embarrass us with pictures from summer camp and old Halloween costumes. It didn't work, and we took it all in stride, while Miles kept reaching for my hand under the blanket we shared on the couch.

At one point, his mom leaned over and said quietly, "You look happy."

"I am," I told her.

She smiled, like that was all she needed to hear.

My dad was more understated, but I saw the way he looked at us. He'd always liked Miles.

And that was enough reassurance for me.

The day grew later as we all sat around the table for hours, playing board games and going through too much coffee in one sitting. My dad made a toast about time and family, and how sometimes life takes you the long way just to bring you home again. My mom kept the wine flowing. The food never seemed to run out. It wasn't loud or chaotic. It was just right.

At one point, I leaned back and looked around the room at everything before me. Miles, laughing with my dad about who knows what, my mom, trying to convince Miles' sister to take home more leftovers, Winter curled up at my feet under the table, the two copies of my novel resting on the side table in the living room.

This was the kind of day we used to imagine but never quite believed we'd get to have.

And now it was ours.

The drive back from Portland was quiet. The roads were mostly empty, the sky already dark by the time we pulled into the driveway.

Winter and Lola were asleep in the back seat, worn out from the chaos of a house full of people. Miles turned off the ignition, glanced at me, and smiled.

"We survived," he said softly.

"Barely," I joked, reaching for the leftovers in the back. "I think we have enough ham and pasta to keep us going through hibernation."

He laughed, then reached over and touched my hand, holding it for a second longer than necessary. But I didn't mind.

Inside, the house felt warmer than I remembered. The Christmas tree still glowed in the corner of the living room, casting a soft light across the hardwood floors. We didn't bother turning on any other lamps, just lit a few candles and set the tone. The fireplace was already crackling. Thankfully, Miles had set the timer that morning to turn it on, so the air smelled faintly of cedar and cinnamon. It was the perfect way to come home.

I kicked off my boots, shrugged off my coat, and went into the kitchen to make tea while Miles let the dogs out one last time. The quiet felt earned tonight. After all the noise and laughter and movement of the day, it was exactly what I needed.

We sat on the couch, legs stretched out, the dogs curled up at our feet. Miles leaned into me, his arm draped casually around my shoulder, his hand resting just beneath my collarbone. He wasn't saying much, and neither was I. But the stillness between us wasn't empty. It was full of everything we'd lived through to get here.

After a while, he stood and disappeared down the hall without a word. I watched him go, unsure of what he was doing or why I suddenly felt my pulse quicken.

When he came back, he was holding a small box that had been wrapped in plain brown paper and tied with a piece of twine, simple but careful, like he'd done it himself.

He held it out to me.

I hesitated. "We said no more gifts."

"I lied," he said softly. "Open it."

My hands trembled as I undid the knot and peeled back the paper. Inside the box was a ring.

One perfect cushion-cut diamond, delicately perched on a slender rose gold band. It was exactly right.

"Miles—" I started, in awe of it.

It caught the light for a moment, glinting with effortless beauty.

I looked up, and he was already down on one knee. "I know it's taken us time to get here. And maybe we didn't follow the path most people do, but I don't want to spend another moment without you. You're it, Keira. And I've known it since the first moment I saw you, since before we even knew what love was."

I didn't say anything at first. I just stared at him, at the ring, at the life we'd built from nothing but memory and hope and second chances.

Then I nodded.

"Yes," I said. "Of course, yes. A thousand times, yes."

He exhaled, like he'd been holding his breath since the moment I walked back into that bookstore in Chicago.

When he slipped the ring onto my finger, my hands were shaking.

The fire crackled, the tree lights blinked slow behind us, and his hand found mine.

This was the ending we never saw coming.

And the beginning we'd always been meant for.

THE END

Acknowledgements

I'd like to begin by thanking my son. Being a stay-at-home mom has given me the rare gift of time and the freedom to discover just how deeply I love writing. I'm grateful every day for the chance to begin this journey with him by my side.

I also want to thank my wonderful husband, who has stood beside me through every step of this process and supported me without hesitation, who believes in me even on the days I struggle to believe in myself.

To my incredible team of beta readers—thank you for helping me shape Miles and Keira into the characters they were meant to be. I truly couldn't have done it without you.

To my best friend, Olga, thank you for being my constant cheerleader, for championing every dream I chase, and for indulging in our endless conversations about book boyfriends. I am so grateful for you.

To my parents, thank you for placing books in my hands, reading to me every night, and raising me among the shelves of bookstores and school libraries. You gave me my love for stories long before I knew I would write my own.

To my fantastic editor, thank you for your work and for helping me become a better writer with every draft.

Thank you to my readers, who have given this little indie book a chance. This is just one of many and I hope you continue to follow me on this journey.

And finally, I want to thank *my* Miles. Thank you for being a part of my life and for inspiring me enough to close one chapter and open another.

About the Author

K. L. Sawyer is an indie author from the beautiful coastal town of Marblehead, Massachusetts. She's a loving wife, a proud boy mom, and a lifelong lover of words who finds peace in both reading and writing.

When she's not working on her next novel, she's dreaming of one day opening a bakery that doubles as a bookshop on the Northshore of Massachusetts, where she can sip on London Fogs and watch the boats go by with her husband and son.